I0641273

Rising Star

The Billionaires' Club Series: Book 5

AE Moran

The Invisible Publishing Company

Copyright © 2025 by A.E. Moran

All rights reserved.

No portion of this book may be reproduced in any form without written permission from the publisher or author, except as permitted by U.S. copyright law.

The Billionaires' Club Series

Contents

Chapter 1: Vivian

I pick up a stack of files and carry them in my elbow on my way to the conference room, but I have to hustle back to my desk when my phone rings for the thousandth time.

I pick it up and answer it. "Welcome to Cast Iron Securities," I announce. "You're speaking with Vivian. How can I help you today?"

"I'm calling about an insurance policy I purchased yesterday," a man's voice tells me. "I want to cancel it."

"I'm sorry to hear that, Sir. If you tell me which salesperson you purchased the policy from, I can transfer you to that person and I'm sure they'll be more than happy to assist you."

The guy's voice spikes with tension. "The salesperson was Ian Fawcett, but I don't want to talk to him. I want to talk to David Newman. He runs Cast Iron Securities, doesn't he?"

"Yes, he does, but I'm afraid he's just going into a meeting at the moment. I can take your name and number and have him call you back in about an hour."

"Yeah, you do that," the guy snaps. "And while you're at it, you can tell him that Ian Fawcett screwed me over! He lied about the cost of the policy and the amount of coverage it provided. He left key details out of his sales pitch so I would sign and buy the policy. He had to send the full prospectus to me afterward. That's how I found out. A guy like that shouldn't be selling any kind of financial instrument."

I cringe. "I really appreciate you telling me. I will definitely pass that on to David. I'm sure he'll be glad you brought this to his attention. This isn't the first time David has caught Ian doing something like this."

The guy changes his tone immediately. "Really? Wow. That's bad. I didn't know that."

"Would you mind giving me your name and number? I'm sure David will want to follow up with you later today. We will definitely cancel your policy....." I hesitate. "And I know David plans to take action with Ian very soon."

"Oh, okay. My name is Alex Rickenbach." He gives me his phone number. I scribble it on the back of my hand. "Thanks. I really appreciate it."

"No problem," I tell him. "I assure you Cast Iron Securities takes these things very seriously. I'm going into the meeting with David now. I'll tell him right now and I'm sure he'll call you as soon as he comes out of the meeting."

"Thanks. I really appreciate it."

"No problem at all. If you're still looking for an insurance policy, I'm sure David can talk to you about some of our other products that would meet your needs."

"That would be great. Thanks." He gets off the phone.

I take a deep breath and make a command decision to power off my phone so I don't get interrupted by another call before the meeting starts.

I pick up my files and race to the conference room just as David and the salespeople show up. David hobnobs with them for a while before we get down to business.

I have to interrupt their conversation to pull David out of the room and give him a rundown on the phone call I just had.

David is a middle-aged guy with jet-black hair and tiny streaks of grey right above his ears. He has a huge personality, a loud voice, big, broad shoulders, and a steamroller attitude toward life in general.

He always wears immaculately tailored suits and he keeps his personal presentation just as refined. He's one of the classiest businessmen I've ever met and he's always bursting with energy.

He reminds me of J. Jonah Jameson from *Spiderman*. He intimidates people who don't know him well, but he has a heart of gold and always does the right thing.

He reacts to the call exactly the way I expect him to. He sucks air between his teeth, puts his hands on his hips, and turns away. "Shit!" he growls.

"This is nothing you didn't already know, right? It doesn't really change anything, does it?"

"No, it doesn't, but it doesn't help, either." He throws up his hands. "I don't need this right now. I'll deal with it later."

"Just make sure you call Alex back after the meeting. He did say he was still interested in buying an insurance policy as long as it was above board. You have to tell him how you're handling this and make sure to sell him a policy he's happy with. Don't let this slip away."

"Right. Of course not." David turns back to the conference room, but right then, a bunch of other salespeople show up for the staff meeting.

David and I stand at the entrance and let them enter first. They all shake hands with David before they file into the room.

The rest of them ignore me. I'm just David's administrative clerk. Most of the salespeople would rather pretend I don't exist—or at least that I'm not as important to the company as they are.

David is the exception. He always tells me how much he appreciates me. He always says he couldn't run this company without me—which is true.

The salespeople greet and shake hands with each other next.

David and I follow them inside, take our places at the head of the table, and David raises his voice. "Take your seats, all of you! Let's get this party started."

The others laugh and move toward their seats. They're just getting settled when a different man enters the room. I've never seen him before.

He's tall, thin, has black hair, and blue eyes. I can't tell how old he. I don't see any grey hair or wrinkles. He just looks worn out and exhausted. Dark circles surround his bloodshot eyes.

His suit doesn't fit him well and it looks like it has seen better days, too. His hair has been cut recently in a short, neat, business style, but that's the only thing about him that looks taken care of.

The other salespeople occupy all the chairs at the table, so he has nowhere to sit. He stops next to the doorway and then moves a few steps inward. He takes a position near the back wall and remains standing.

David gives the guy a hard look and then pretends he isn't there. The salespeople all turn around to look at the stranger. Their expressions tell me none of them recognize him, either.

David distracts everyone into facing the front. "I'm sure you're all as excited about this month's staff meeting as I am, so let's not beat around the bush."

Laughter breaks out. "I'm so excited I'm pissing myself back here," Isaac Steinman interrupts.

"We have bathrooms down the hall for that," David tells him. "Don't do it in here or you'll be paying to clean the chairs."

"Give us the sales rankings for the month," Rowan Barrymore interjects. "Don't leave us in suspense."

"First things first. I'm sure you all noticed our new salesman." David waves toward the back of the room. "This is Derek Salazar. He'll be joining us starting today."

A hushed murmur races around the room as the other salespeople turn around to look at Derek a second time. He doesn't look like he has two pennies to rub together.

David breaks the uncomfortable silence again by opening his laptop and switching on the big flat screen behind him.

"Now getting to this month's sales rankings.....in first place, we have Ian Fawcett....."

Groans break out all around the table. "Not again!" Rowan snarls.

"That's impossible!" Isaac snaps. "There aren't enough people in New Jersey for him to sell insurance policies to."

Ian laughs. He's a tall, strapping lady-killer with highlighted blonde hair and a crazy, devil-may-care grin.

He pushes back his chair. "Read 'em and weep, suckers. I'm the best and I always will be."

Grumbles follow him to the front of the room. He strides up to David grinning like anything and holds out his hand to shake.

David shakes his hand and pulls Ian in to stand next to him. David puts his hand on Ian's shoulder and turns him around to face the room. Here it comes.

"Ian sold thirty insurance policies, fifteen investment instruments, and seven securities portfolios this month," David goes on. "He sold almost forty percent more than Rowan, who comes in at second place."

"Bastard," Rowan mutters and makes Ian laugh again.

No one else says anything. The salespeople all glare at Ian.

"We also uncovered evidence that ten of the insurance policies were sold under fraudulent terms," David goes on. "He misrepresented both the cost and coverage amounts of these policies and half the investment instruments belonged to discredited or, in some cases, non-existent investments that would channel investment funds into an offshore account with Ian's name on them."

Ian jumps out of his skin and spins around fast. "What?! I never did any of that! You can't prove I did anything wrong! You're all just jealous."

David waves to me. I hand over the files I've been holding in my arms all this time.

He puts the stack on the table and starts opening them one after the other. "We have cases of similar fraud and malfeasance going back six months. In fact, we just got another complaint from a customer this morning that you did the same thing yesterday. Does the name Alex Rickenbach mean anything to you?"

All the color drains from Ian's face. He stares at David and then Ian's eyes dart out to the rest of his fellow salespeople.

"You're fired," David tells him. "You have ten minutes to clean out your desk and vacate the premises. I've already reported you to the SEC and handed over all this evidence. You might want to go home and put your affairs in order."

Ian gulps, takes one last wild look around, and beats it out of the room. Another tense silence falls over the group after he leaves.

David inhales a deep breath and puffs out his cheeks in exasperation. At least that part is over with.

"So....getting back to the business at hand....Rowan is our first-place sales finisher this month......" David pushes a button on his computer and deletes Ian's name and sales data from the screen.

Cheers break out around the table along with plenty of relieved laughter. Everyone claps Rowan on the back before he stands up, comes to the front of the room, and David hands him a fat bonus check.

They shake hands. Rowan won't stop beaming and his cheeks color. David turns him around to face the room and everyone hoots, whistles, and applauds him.

"That's all we have to cover today," David yells over the noise. "You'll all receive this month's leads in your email. Let's get out there and get it done."

The meeting breaks up. The salespeople crowd around Rowan, congratulate him, and everyone talks much more excitedly about the prospect of competing against him and each other, now that Ian is gone.

No one notices or tries to include Derek. He stands off to one side watching and listening. He doesn't come forward to introduce himself or break the ice.

David mutters, "I better go call Alex," and leaves the room.

He stops off at the doorway to exchange a few words with Derek and then David beats it.

That leaves Derek here alone with a bunch of strangers.

Chapter 2: Vivian

I pick up the stack of files from the table along with David's laptop. I'll take it back to his office, but I'll wait until he gets off the phone first.

I don't envy him having to tell Alex what happened. I'm glad Ian is gone. He cast a cloud over the whole company.

I head for the door to go back to my desk. I have to pass Derek on the way there.

I stop and hold out my hand. "Welcome aboard," I tell him. "I'm Vivian Cooper. I'm the administrative clerk for Cast Iron Securities. I'm sure I'll be seeing a lot of you around here in the coming days."

He nods and shakes my hand. God, he looks so sad and depressed! "It's nice to meet you," he murmurs.

"Would you like me to show you around the office? You probably want to settle in at your desk and get started swimming with these sharks." I jerk my thumb over my shoulder at the other salespeople.

He doesn't register even a twinge of a smile. "You don't have to. David showed me around when he interviewed me."

I frown at him. David never told me he was interviewing another salesperson. I would definitely remember that. I'm the one who has to process all the paperwork when we bring on new staff.

I wave at nothing. "I better get back to work, then. It was nice to meet you. I'm sure I'll see you around."

I head out of the conference room. He follows me and gets ready to turn off in the other direction.

My desk sits outside of David's office where he can call me if he needs me and also so salespeople and anyone else who wants to see him have to go through me first.

The salespeople's cubicles fill the office's central floor. More offices surround the floor. The consistent high sellers usually get assigned to those offices, but no one works in them now. Ian was on his way to earning one of those offices, but not anymore.

Derek turns toward the cubicles. I plan to go back to my desk and check to see if David assigned Derek his own cubicle yet.

Neither of us gets anywhere before the other salespeople come out of the conference room. They all talk, laugh, jostle each other around, and talk about making plans to meet up after work.

Rowan spots Derek. "Hey—the new guy!" He holds out his hand. "We totally didn't expect David to bring on a new person—but then again, none of us saw that coming with Ian."

"Thanks," Derek mumbles. "I'm just happy to be here."

Another chill falls over the group. He doesn't look happy about anything. He looks like a loser.

He won't be able to sell much when he looks like this. The potential customers won't be able to take him seriously—and neither will the other salespeople.

Rowan tries to thaw the ice. "So.....did you work somewhere else before this?"

David comes back before Derek has a chance to answer. David passes his hand across his eyes. "I just talked to Alex. He is interested in another policy, but he doesn't want to do it today. You can take that one, Rowan. You deserve it."

"Thanks, man," Rowan replies. "I'll make sure take to good care of him."

"I know you will." David furrows his brow at Derek. "Have you met everyone? This is Isaac Steinman, Rowan Barrymore, Ellie Shelton, and this is our administrative clerk, Vivian Cooper."

Derek shakes hands with everyone he hasn't already shaken hands with. He repeats again that it's nice to meet everyone.

David bumps Derek's shoulder before anyone can ask Derek any more questions. "Come with me and I'll show you which cubicle is yours."

David and Derek leave together. The salespeople start whispering to each other about how beaten down and disheveled Derek looks.

"I can't believe David gave him a job," Isaac murmurs.

"Maybe David just wanted to bring someone in to replace Ian until he finds a real salesman."

I don't listen to anything else. I go to my desk and then put David's laptop on his desk in his office.

I refile the folders I pulled for the meeting. Then I have to get busy entering a bunch of data and doing a bunch of other paperwork—including Derek's employment paperwork.

I find myself looking up at him across the office. He's a mystery and he keeps it that way by acting so quiet and reserved. He really won't be able to sell anything if he acts like that around the customers.

I turn back to my work, but when I start to enter his employment details, I find some information missing. This is what I get for letting the boss handle this without me.

I stand up to go over to Derek's cubicle, but he's already gone. The other salespeople stand around the water cooler talking. None of them has even checked their leads for the month.

So Derek is a go-getter after all. He's out there beating the bricks before anyone else. Maybe he knows something the rest of them don't.

I put his employment paperwork aside for later. I'll ask him after he comes back to the office. Heaven knows I have enough to do apart from that.

The other salespeople leave to go hunt down their next sales. The SEC calls for David and then sends over one of their officers to go over the evidence against Ian. I forget all about Derek in the commotion.

David slumps behind his desk after it's all over. "What a mess this is turning out to be," he growls.

"Why didn't you tell me you hired Derek?" I ask. "If I didn't know any better, I would say you were trying to hide something from me."

"I was trying to hide it from Ian. I wanted to humiliate him in front of everyone. If I told you about Derek, the rest of the office would have found out and the news could have gotten back to him. I wanted to spring it on him." He waves that away. "I'm sure I can hire people in my own company without consulting you."

"It isn't that. I just thought you would have confided in me."

He turns away. "Now you know why I didn't."

Those words dismiss the subject. He's right. He doesn't have to consult me about anything.

I head back to my desk just as the salespeople file in. They gather around the water cooler to talk about how much luck they had with their customers today.

They're still standing there in between occasional trips to their desks. Derek doesn't come in until five-thirty when everyone is getting ready to leave.

His arrival causes another commotion. The others crowd in to surround his cubicle. "How did it go?" Rowan asks. "Did you have any luck?"

Derek takes a stack of manila envelopes out of a heavy-duty leather business satchel he carries over his shoulder. The bag looks well-built—and expensive. It conflicts with every other impression I've been getting from him.

He holds up the envelopes and lays them on his desk. "Seven closes."

Everyone in the group gasps and their jaws drop. "Seven?!" Isaac exclaims. "No, you didn't!"

Derek turns his back on them. "I gotta log these in. How did you all do?"

They won't stop staring at him. One sales closure a day is really good. That was Ian's average and he only accomplished that by cheating the system. Seven is unheard of, but Derek plays it off like it's nothing.

The others take a long time to pick their jaws up off the floor. He starts tapping on his computer and pretends the other salespeople aren't there.

The other salespeople exchange glances and then Rowan gulps to get his voice working. "Hey.....man.....just tell us.....You must have worked in sales before."

Derek replies over his shoulder. "Yeah, I have."

"Well......where did you work?" Isaac asked. "Maybe we know some of the people you worked with."

"I worked in New York," Derek replies.

He shows no other acknowledgment of their reaction. They shuffle their feet and then exchange glances.

They would congratulate anyone else in the office who accomplished so much. Some of those salespeople might even ask him how he did it.

None of them asks or even says anything. They all end up wandering away to their own cubicles and then leave for the evening.

He sits at his desk for a long time working. He and I are the last people left in the office.

I finally muster up the courage to take my tablet and go over there. He stops what he's doing to turn around and face me.

"Excuse me," I begin. "I need to fill in some gaps in your employment paperwork. David didn't tell me he was hiring you. He wanted to keep your employment a secret so he could fire Ian publicly."

Derek nods. "I know. He told me."

My eyes shoot up to meet his. "He told you?! You knew he was going to fire Ian?"

He nods again. "He told me the whole story. He said he needed to hire someone to take Ian's place right away and didn't want anyone else in the office to find out I was starting the same day."

I gape at him in shock. He knew. Derek is the only person David told. Does this mean something?

Derek snaps me out of my trance. "What do you need me to fill out?"

"Oh, right!" I jump out of my skin, step into his cubicle, and put the tablet down on the desk in front of him. "I just need your Social Security number, designated receiving bank account number, prior employment experience, emergency contact details, and your signature at the bottom."

I scroll on the screen and point out each place one after the other.

He enters all the information, signs on the dotted line, and hands me the tablet back. "Is there anything else you need from me?"

I find myself frowning at him. "I heard you before when you said you've done sales before."

He sits there staring up at me while he waits for me to say something. "Yeah?"

"The prior experience you entered into this form isn't in New York. It's in Pennsylvania."

He doesn't move. "Yeah? What's your question?"

I study him even more closely if that's possible. I might as well be talking to a brick wall. He won't tell me anything.

I mumble, "Never mind," go back to my desk, and enter the rest of his information into the company employment files.

I go over his information with a fine-toothed comb. I'm still doing it when I find an email from David in my inbox. It includes all the information Derek gave David to get this job, including Derek's resume and application form.

The resume doesn't include any sales experience in New York, either. All of it is more than fifteen years old and it's all from Pennsylvania.

Derek sold financial instruments there, too, but that begs the question. What did he do in those fifteen years?

Where has he been hiding and what has he been doing that could lead him all the way down here to the deepest, darkest, most forgotten, bottommost corner of New Jersey?

Chapter 3: Derek

I turn a corner and stop to check my phone for directions to my prospect's office. The prospective customer is the owner of fourteen McDonald's franchises in this area. He wants to buy insurance policies for his franchises.

This could be the biggest sale I make yet. I have to land this customer.

I freeze in my tracks when I see Jackson Metcalf and Dante Helme coming toward me. I haven't seen either of them since I left New York.

They both look as crisp and impressive as ever. They both wear expensive tailored suits and Jackson wears the Rolex I've been seeing him wear for years. These guys understand classic style and they show their class in everything they do.

Seeing them makes me realize how down on my luck I am. I look like life dragged me through the gutter, which it did.

I at least have the backbone to stop where I am and wait for them to pull up in front of me.

"Hey, man," Jackson murmurs.

I decide to take the bull by the horns. "You guys are a little out of your way, aren't you? I'm sure you both have better things to do than to hang around in a small town like this—unless you're planning to buy it."

"We came down here to see you," Dante replies. "None of us is happy about the way things worked out."

"I'm sure Lane Prince and all the executives from Apico Acquisitions are happy about the way things worked out." I can't stop the bitterness from creeping into my voice. "They robbed me of everything. I built Titanium Finance with my own two hands and they snuck in and snatched it out from under me. I'm here because of them."

"Lane isn't happy about what happened to you," Jackson replies. "He never wanted you to end up here. He tried to include you in the merger...."

"It wasn't a merger!" I snap. "It was a hostile takeover. You can't expect me to stand around having a bunch of strangers rub it in my face that they made me an employee in my own company. None of you guys would put up with that, either. You wouldn't stand for it."

Jackson looks away. Of course none of the guys from The Billionaires' Club would put up with that. Every last one of them would have walked away with nothing before they suffered that kind of public humiliation, which is exactly what I did.

"What do you want?" I growl under my breath. "I'm on my way to an important meeting. Say what you have to say and leave me alone. I don't want to be late."

"We want you to come back to New York," Dante tells me. "We'll stake you in your next venture. You can get back everything you lost. You don't have to torture yourself in this purgatory."

Now I'm the one who looks away. I shake my head. "I won't accept any handouts from anyone. If I get back what I lost, I'll do it on my own."

"You don't have to do this," Jackson exclaims. "You don't have to do everything alone."

"Yes, I do. I built Titanium Finance alone and I'll rebuild this alone. Nothing can stop me as long as I stick to it—and this time, I'll make sure no one ever takes it away from me."

"So you are planning something," Dante added. "I knew it. What is it? At least give us an idea of what you're planning."

"I don't think so. This is all mine. I don't want anyone else involved and I don't want to share the profits with any other investors. Now I gotta go. You gentlemen have a good day."

I don't give them a chance to say another word. I side-step around them and keep walking. In a minute, I duck into the prospect's building and shut the door behind me.

I take a few minutes to collapse there against the wall and catch my breath. Cold sweat stings me all over.

I don't want anyone from New York knowing where I am or what I'm doing. I especially don't want anyone from The Billionaires' Club knowing where I am or what I'm doing.

I don't even really care if Lane Prince is laughing all the way to the bank while he makes a killing off the company I built.

I don't care about anything except rebuilding my empire—my bulletproof empire this time.

I'll build something bigger and more profitable than Titanium ever was. This enterprise will be totally impenetrable. It will be a fortress that no one can ever get their dirty little hands on. I'll make certain of it

.

I pull myself together, climb the stairs, and enter my prospect's office. I leave with the sale under my belt and head back to my car.

I'm just walking around the corner when a beautiful young woman steps out of a nearby office supply store.

She stops in her track and stares at me. She's stunningly gorgeous with strawberry-blonde hair with red tints in it. Her clear green eyes widen when she sees me. It's Vivian Cooper, the admin clerk from Cast Iron Securities.

She always wears pencil skirts with a flared ruffle around the hem. She shows off her magnificent hourglass figure with tight cardigans or a crop top tied in a bow in the front. Her shapely legs angle down to tall pink heels on her feet.

She always looks timeless, classy, and perfectly put together. A woman as delicious as that wouldn't look sideways at a penniless nobody like me.

"Hi!" she greets me.

"Hi," I murmur back. I want to get away from her.

"How are you doing?" she asks. "How are your sales going?"

I keep my tone flat. I don't want her thinking I'm trying to talk to her. "They're going fine. Thanks for asking."

"Do you need anything? Did you just see Ryan Schwartzbauer?"

I nod. "I just finished talking to him."

"How did that go?"

"Fine," I reply.

She finally gets the message and stops to stare at me. How much longer do I have to stand here before I can make a tactful exit?

She finally shakes herself and waves over her shoulder at nothing. "I just saw you talking to Jackson Metcalfe and Dante Helme earlier. Do you know them?"

I shrug. "I know of them."

"It's pretty unusual to see billionaires like that this far south. They usually stick to New York. Maybe they were down here doing business."

"I guess so," I mumble.

"Did they say anything about it to you? Did they mention why they came down this far south?"

"They didn't say," I lie. "I better go. I have a few other prospects to meet today. I'll see you back at the office."

She bursts into a beautiful smile. She's stunning. "Okay. Have a good day."

I mumble, "You, too," and walk another thirty feet to my car.

She stands there watching me while I get in and drive away. I'm driving a secondhand 1992 Toyota Camry that has seen better days. Everything I own right now has seen better days—all except my leather satchel.

I bought it for myself when I first started Titanium Finance. I had to sell all my nice suits, electronics, cars, penthouse, and every other nice thing I had when I left New York, but I kept this satchel for myself. I'll never part with it.

It represents all the work I put into building that company. I did it once. I can do it again. Anyone who gets in my way will live to regret it.

Chapter 4: Vivian

I carry the usual stack of file folders into the conference room, set up David's laptop on the table, and make sure it's hooked up to the display screen. I'm still tapping on it when Derek comes in.

I look up and find myself smiling at him. He's a fixture around the office after working for Cast Iron Securities for three and a half weeks. "Hello there," I greet him. "The meeting isn't starting yet. You don't have to be here."

"I just finished logging my latest closes. I don't have anything else to do." He sits down in one of the chairs near the other end of the table. "I figured I would get here before the rest of the herd eats all the donuts."

I laugh at him. "That's funny, but if you want donuts, you have to bring them yourself. David is a health nut. He doesn't believe in using company time to promote such poor eating habits."

"I agree with him." He swivels his chair around. "At least I get to sit in a real chair this time instead of standing in the back like the problem child."

I laugh again. This is the most he has come out of his shell since he started working here.

He has been warming up to the other salespeople more and more as they get to know him, but he still keeps his distance. He makes casual conversation, but he never tells anyone anything about himself, especially not anything about his recent past.

The mystery of why he left New York has been burning a hole in the back of my mind.

I'm not the only one. The salespeople have started a betting pool to see who can guess why he's here and who he really is.

So far, the real money is on a nefarious criminal past. Some even speculate that murder is involved. Others think he might have suffered a catastrophic divorce or maybe even a head injury that caused him to lose his memory.

I'm not involved in the pool and I don't plan to be. I keep track of all the theories, though. I really want to find out Derek's story. My curiosity is killing me.

David comes in just then and claps Derek on the shoulder. "You don't have to be in here yet, buddy. You can chill."

"That's what I'm doing," Derek replies. "It's more chill in here with Vivian than it is out there with Larry, Curly, and Moe."

David laughs. "Tell me about it." He comes up to the front of the room and fiddles with his computer. I have to go back to my desk to get a few things.

All the salespeople are in the conference room taking their seats by the time I get back. Their talk drowns out everything else until David gets their attention.

"Let's get started so you can all get back out there and do what you do best," David begins. "Does anyone have any questions or business to raise before we announce this month's sales rankings?"

"Why bother?" Rowan asks. "We all know Derek blew us out of the water."

"He's as bad as Ian," Isaac adds. "I hope you checked his sales to make sure they're legit."

"They are," David replies. "I contacted all his customers to follow up. That's part of the probationary period for any new sales associate coming to work here. All the customers are thrilled with the packages they got. I guess we don't need to go through the formalities if you all already know the results."

He switches on his computer to display the sales numbers on the screen behind him.

"Come on up, Derek," David tells him. "You deserve it."

Derek goes up to the front of the room. Certain people shake his hand and congratulate him on the way there.

He shakes David's hand and David gives him the hefty bonus check the highest sales earner receives every month.

"Thanks," Derek murmurs.

David goes through the usual routine of clapping Derek on the shoulder, turning him toward the table, and going over everyone's sales numbers. Isaac is right. Derek smoked them all.

The meeting breaks up with the usual banter. Derek joins in some of it, but as always, he never lets anything personal slip out.

He doesn't have any problem making the others laugh, but he doesn't laugh much himself. He always stays serious and reserved even when he's surrounded by people smiling at him.

"We're going out for drinks after work today," Ellie tells him. "You should come with us. Come on. Don't tell me you're keeping kidnapped prisoners tied up in your basement somewhere. When are you going to come with us for a change?"

His lips twitch, but he stops himself from smiling. "All right. I'll come. I suppose the prisoners can go without food for a few more hours."

The others laugh some more, but I can't help watching him. What if he *is* keeping tortured, kidnapped prisoners tied up in his basement?

What if that's the real reason he had to leave New York—because he's on the run from the law?

I don't want to believe that, but anything is possible. No one here knows anything about Derek. The resume he submitted to get this job doesn't tell me anything about his personal life.

He intrigues me, but I also find myself liking him. He's always controlled, always polite and considerate, and never takes it the wrong way when the other salespeople give him a hard time for keeping his life such a secret from us.

We go about our business until the end of work. David is going out for drinks with the salespeople, too. I probably wouldn't be able to go if he didn't go.

We meet up at a pool hall down the street and get a big table in the back where we can all talk as loudly as we want to without disturbing anyone.

We wouldn't be disturbing anyone because everyone here talks loudly. "Derek is buying drinks tonight, everyone," Rowan announces. "He can afford it out of that big bonus and he owes it to the rest of us."

"He doesn't own you squat, man," David cuts in. "He earned that bonus, so don't think you're going to rob him of it now." He chops his hand at Derek. "I'll buy the drinks."

"Tell us how you did it," Ellie tells Derek. "I've never seen a salesman who can close like you do. What's your secret?"

"Appeal to the prospect's self-interest," Derek replies.

"How do we do that when we're the ones trying to sell them something?" Isaac asks.

"Find out why they want the product and what their needs are," Derek replies. "Then show them how the product fits their needs. Then they feel like they have to buy it."

"How do we find that out?" Ellie asks.

"You ask them questions beforehand." Derek frowns at her and then at everyone else at the table. "Are you seriously sitting there telling me you don't ask the prospect questions beforehand?"

The others exchange glances.

"What do you do if you don't ask questions?" Derek shuts his eyes and shakes his head. "I shouldn't even be asking."

"We sell them the product, of course," Rowan points out. "We pitch the products' features and advantages."

"But you don't know what features and advantages the prospect needs if you don't ask them first," Derek counters. "You might be pitching a product on price when the prospect is more concerned about security."

No one says anything for a minute. That sure killed the conversation.

"You can't know what the prospect wants or why they might even want to buy that product if you don't ask them first and find out what they're looking for." Derek frowns at them all again. "This is basic sales 101. Don't you know that?"

Rowan picks up his drink. "You'll have to show us."

"Just try it. Talk to your prospects first, find out what they need, and then sell them what they need. It's simple."

"Where did you learn all of this?" Ellie asks. "Did you learn it in New York?"

"No, I learned it selling comic books to the kids on my block in South Philly." Derek shuts his mouth real quick and hides behind his drink. He pretends he never said that.

A silence falls over the table when everyone realizes he actually said something about his past.

David comes to the rescue. "So how about Ryan Schwartzbauer signing all those franchises, huh? That was a haul. I never thought anyone would land that whale."

Derek shrugs. "He was just a sale like any other."

"He called me today and said he contacted some other franchisees who want insurance. I think it's only fair that those leads should go to you."

"Hey, man!" Isaac cuts in. "What about the rest of us? He's already rolling in the clover. Throw us a bone for a change."

"Go find your own bone," David fires back. "He earned this. We wouldn't have these leads if not for him. He's the only salesman here I can trust to actually close these deals. Pull up your socks and you'll reap the fruits of your effort the same way he is now."

"I don't mind passing them on," Derek replies. "I have too many leads this month already."

"We don't need your charity," Isaac snarls.

"You just asked me for charity," David points out. "Make up your mind. Are you doing your own work or not?"

Derek pushes back his chair. "I better go. Thank you for inviting me. This was great. I'll see you all back at the office."

"Stick around," David tells him. "The night is young."

"My prisoners will be getting anxious." Derek downs the rest of his drink. "See ya."

He walks off.

"Now look what you did," David snaps as soon as Derek gets out of earshot. "Don't you ever stop complaining about your own incompetence?"

"Hey!" Isaac counters. "I pull my weight."

"That's all you do. You do the bare minimum to pay your bills and then you have the nerve to bitch and moan about a man who breaks his back and performs so high above your level you can't even understand his methods. I swear, if I hear you sniping about his results again, I'm going to have to seriously question if you even belong in this organization."

Isaac gasps out loud. "You can't do that!"

"I can just as easily give your leads to him as give them to you. One thing I am certain of. He will be able to close them all, which is more than I can say for you. If I was in your place, I would be less concerned with what he's doing and more concerned about doing your own job."

"I can't believe he actually told us how he does it," Ellie exclaims. "He could have kept it to himself and continued to sweep the results every month. He didn't have to do that."

"That's because he's a straight-up guy," David replies. "I keep telling you, but you won't believe it. I double-checked every sale. He's honest, straightforward, and does everything above board. His customers think he's the greatest. Some of them even invited him over to have dinner with their families."

"No way!" Rowan breathes.

"You should all spend some time learning from him. He obviously knows a lot more about sales than we do."

Chapter 5: Vivian

I step out of the bar into a blast of freezing cold wind. It cuts straight through my clothes.

I pull my heavy wool coat tighter around my body, but nothing protects me from the waist down. I'm only wearing this thin skirt and my heels.

I stumble away from the bar heading back to the office where I left my car in the parking lot. I fumble for my keys on the way there. I don't want any delays to stop me from getting in the car and turning on the heater.

It's already dark by the time I leave the bar. I could have asked David to walk me back, but he's still in there drinking and talking to the other salesmen. I don't want to wait any longer. I'm tired and I want to go home.

I shiver in the cold. The wind hits me in the face and numbs my lips. I need to get inside quickly.

I clutch my keys in my hand, round a corner, and step into the halo of a streetlight over the parking lot. All the salespeople's cars are still there. So is Derek's.

I look around when I notice it. He can't still be here. He left hours ago.

That's when I notice a light on inside the office. He's still in there working in his cubicle. Wow. That's dedication for you. None of the others would do that. Not even David does that.

I can't stand around staring. I head for my car—and stop in my tracks when I see that I have a flat tire.

I curse under my breath. This is the last thing I need.

I'm not even sure if I can change the tire when my hands are so numb. I drop my keys once before I get the door open.

I sit inside the driver's compartment, start the motor, and warm up in the heater while I muster up the courage to go back out there and change the tire. I really don't want to spend my evening doing that, but I have no choice.

I take a deep breath, get out, storm around to the trunk, take everything out of the toolbox, and lay out the jack and tire iron next to the tire.

The spare hangs underneath the chassis. The tools include a crank to unwind the spare and lower it to the ground.

I squat down, pull the tools out, and try to figure out how to assemble the crank so I can get to the spare. I'm just repositioning the jigsaw of pieces when Derek comes out of the building.

"What are you.....oh. You have a flat." He comes over to me. "Go sit in the car. I'll do this for you."

"You don't have to do that," I tell him. "My dad would have a fit if he found out I let some guy change my tire for me."

Derek actually smiles at me for the first time. "I won't tell him if you don't. Go get in the car. You aren't dressed for this."

I cast a glance at his tousled suit. "You aren't, either. You don't even have a coat."

"My mom would roll in her grave if she knew I let some helpless woman in high heels change a tire in this wind without trying to help. Go on. Your face is turning blue."

I have to laugh. "Thank you."

"Stop it. Go on."

I get in the car and slam the door. I'm shaking too badly to care if I'm being independent enough.

The car trembles when Derek lowers the spare, jacks up the car, and then wrenches the tire iron to take off the flat.

I find myself watching him in the side view mirrors. He's such an interesting guy—or maybe it's just his silence that makes him seem interesting.

He stands up and passes his sleeve across his eyes before he comes over to my window. A punishing sheet of freezing wind lashes my face when I roll the window down.

"Pop your trunk so I can put everything away."

I do it. He heaves the spare in there and spends a long time putting all the tools away. He finally comes back to my window.

"There's a twenty-four-hour garage two blocks that way. I'll follow you just to make sure nothing happens on the way and then I'll drive you home."

"Thank you," I tell him. "I really appreciate it."

He stops himself from smiling again. "We'll call it a late-night adventure. You go first and I'll follow."

He gets into his crappy old Camry. He could afford to buy a new car or a new suit with the bonus he got today, but something tells me he won't.

I wait for him to switch on his headlights. Then I pull out of the parking lot and he follows me to the garage.

He comes inside with me while I talk to the mechanic about replacing my tire and putting it back on. He says the car will be ready for me in the morning.

I realize while I'm standing here how much better I feel with Derek here. I'm standing here shivering in an auto shop in the middle of the night. Anything could happen to me.

It won't happen because he's with me. It's a good feeling not to have to worry about that.

I follow Derek back to his car. He surprises me by opening the passenger door for me to get in.

I sit down and finally relax in the rush of warm air coming from the heater. It feels heavenly after the cold outside.

Derek gets in, slams his door, and takes off driving through the night. "My house is on Riverview Terrace," I tell him.

"I know," he replies.

I look up. "How do you know that? How do you know where I live?"

"Because you included your information in the welcome letter you sent me with my employment paperwork, remember?" He glances at me while he drives. "It was right there at the bottom of the page. You said I shouldn't hesitate to call on you if I needed anything."

I look away. "Oh, yeah. I forgot about that."

"I'll wipe it from my memory banks if you want me to."

I snort. "You couldn't."

"No, but it sounded like the right thing to say at the time."

I find myself studying the side of his face. He's actually really good-looking. "You look a lot better. You don't look as drained and beaten down now as you did when you first came to work here. You look like you regained your health."

He doesn't look at me. "This job relieved a lot of stress I was under. I can rebuild my life here, thanks to this job."

"I'm sure you'll be getting a lot more bonuses if you keep going the way you are. Then again, the others might overtake you if you keep giving away all your sales secrets to them."

"I don't have any sales secrets. I didn't tell them anything they couldn't have learned by watching any YouTube video." He scowls at me on the side. "Why don't they talk to you? The salespeople don't include you in their conversations. I don't hear you having conversations with anyone other than David."

I make a face. "The salespeople wouldn't stoop so low as to have a conversation with a lowly support worker like me."

"That's ridiculous. I'm sure you practically run the place. I bet if I asked David he would tell me that he couldn't run the company without you."

I blush. "He says that all the time, but you're right. He's the only one."

He has to go back to looking at the road. "That's stupid. I wouldn't tolerate that if it was my company."

"Well, it isn't your company and it isn't like David can force the salespeople to talk to me."

"He could promote a culture of recognizing the people who make their incomes possible." He compresses his lips. "Never mind. It's none of my business."

"You say that like you have experience with that."

He shakes his head. "I wouldn't tell David how to run his business. I'm sure he does a good job without me."

He pulls up in front of my apartment building just then and we both get out. He walks me up to my door. "Thank you for everything tonight," I tell him. "I'm really grateful."

"I'm just glad you're okay. You'll get your car back tomorrow and everything will be fine."

I smile at him again, say another, "Thank you," and turn away to go inside. He turns in the other direction to go back to his car.

"Hey, Derek!" I blurt out at the last minute.

He turns around. "Hmm?"

"Would you like to go out for coffee sometimes—some time when we aren't working, I mean? Let me reciprocate. I want to."

He smiles again, but it isn't a full, bright beaming smile. I don't even know if he's capable of that.

"Sure," he murmurs. "I would like that, too. Neither of us is working this weekend. Why don't I meet you at the Morning Brew at nine tomorrow?"

I beam at him. "Great. I'll see you then."

Chapter 6: Derek

I pause down the block to check my appearance in my car window. I look as ratty as ever.

I can't decide if I should stay like this or not. I look like the worst salesman of all time, but at least no one thinks to check on who I am. No one finds out where I came from or why.

I shouldn't be meeting Vivian for coffee. I shouldn't let her think this might go somewhere.

I want it to go somewhere. That's the problem. I really like her.

I shouldn't let her find out who I really am, either. It's bad enough I might wind up leaving this area soon—or sooner than I hope. I don't want to lead her on.

This is just coffee. She said she wants to reciprocate after I helped her last night. That's all it is—even though I know it isn't.

She's the only person at Cast Iron Securities that I really want to see. I wouldn't have gone out to have drinks with them if she wasn't going to be there.

She's the bright spot in the whole experience of working there. Does she even know it?

I would bet cold hard cash that David feels the same way, but he never asks her out. He can't. She's his subordinate.

I turn a corner and see her already approaching the coffee shop. She looks as stunning as ever even when she's wearing that heavy woolen overcoat against the cold.

She's wearing another tight-fitting skirt and heels. She's wearing stockings this time, but they only contribute to her usual classy look.

Her hair tosses in the wind before she goes inside all breathless and glowing from the cold. I get the sense again that I'm nowhere near good enough for her.

I wouldn't have hesitated to go after her when I had money. She would have been the first woman I set my sights on.

I can't do that now. I just hope she's still single by the time I make good on all my plans.

Some lucky guy will probably snatch her up before then. The other sales guys are morons if they don't realize what a prize she is.

She's sitting right in front of them day in and day out, but they never notice her. Maybe she's too familiar and they don't even see her anymore.

I walk into the coffee shop and meet her at the table before we both sit down. "Hi!" she pants.

"Hi," I reply. "Did you get your car?"

"I'm going to get it after this."

"I'll drive you," I tell her. "I don't want you walking around in this cold."

I stop myself from saying what I'm really thinking. I can just imagine the effect the cold is having on her body.

I can just imagine all the places on her body that I would warm up with my mouth. I would make her pant like that from something other than cold—but I'm not thinking about that.

She puts her handbag on the floor and pulls off her coat to reveal another tight-fitting shirt tied across her chest and knotted behind her back. Her top makes her breasts stand out like nobody's business.

I have to stop myself from staring at her breasts and cleavage. I focus on her eyes instead which are as interesting if not more so.

"You've been playing the dark horse since you came to work here," she remarks. "Why are you so secretive about your recent past? You know the guys are betting on what crime you committed in New York that made you flee from justice."

I don't take the joke. "Don't you believe the stories about me keeping prisoners in my basement? You should know better than to ask a guy like me out for coffee."

She laughs. She does that a lot around me. She never laughs at the office, but then again, no one at the office tries to make her laugh.

She doesn't join in the salesmen's jokes and witty banter. She watches from a distance. Someone would think she didn't have a sense of humor, but she lets it out around me. Am I the only one?

Her eyes twinkle at me across the table. "Something tells me that, if you kept prisoners in your basement, you would have kidnapped me last night while you had me alone with a flat tire. No one ever would have found out."

Her eyes sparkle with a light I haven't seen in a long time. That's the moment when the truth hits me between the eyes. She likes me.

I like her, too. That's why she's saying this. She knows that, if I was a real psycho, I would want to kidnap her and keep her in my basement for other reasons—not to torture her or cannibalize her flesh.

I do want to kidnap her and cannibalize her flesh, but not in that way. I can think of a lot of things I would do to her, but I would do them in my bedroom, not in the basement.

I'm not thinking about that. The waiter distracts us by showing up, putting mugs and cutlery on our table, and he takes our order. She gets a hot cocoa. I get coffee.

"Why were you at the office last night?" she asks. "You left the bar and went straight back to work."

I look down at the table to make a microscopic adjustment to the position of my fork and butter knife on the napkin. "I had some things I wanted to get done when no one else was around."

"What kind of things?"

I shrug. "Just personal things—nothing work-related."

"Why did you do them at the office, then? Why not do them at home?"

"I don't know. It's quiet at the office...."

"Isn't it quiet at home at ten o'clock at night?"

"It is, but I can concentrate at the office. I've always been like this."

Her eyes drill me with even more intensity. "You've always been like what?"

I find myself shifting in my seat. She sure doesn't leave me anywhere to hide or any way to weasel out of her questions.

"I mean it's always been easier for me to work somewhere other than home. I've always been able to concentrate more if I leave home and go somewhere else—somewhere like an office or something."

"So have you done sales in an office before? You said you learned on the streets of South Philly. I'm guessing you didn't have an office then."

I find myself smiling at her. She makes me want to smile even if some part of me thinks I shouldn't. "No, I didn't have an office then."

"So what did you do? Where did you go when you wanted to leave home and go somewhere else to concentrate?"

The waiter saves me by delivering our drinks just then. He only saves me for a few seconds, though. He leaves me alone with Vivian staring at me across the table.

I decide to deflect all these questions about my past. I really wish I could tell her who I really am and why I came down to this part of New Jersey, but I can't tell her that.

I don't want anyone to know who I am. I could have gone to great lengths to hide my identity. I didn't have to use my real name.

I'm amazed that she or some other curious person hasn't already looked me up and found out the truth. I suppose it's only a matter of time.

"Why did you ask me out to coffee?" I ask instead.

"Why wouldn't I? You were really nice to me last night—much nicer than anyone at the office has been to me in all the years I've been working there combined."

"Has any of them ever seen you standing in the freezing wind trying to change a flat tire?"

"No, but seven years is a long time to treat someone like they aren't there."

My head shoots up. "You've been there for seven years?!"

I nod. "Why does that surprise you?"

I look down at my coffee so I can add milk and sugar to it. "I didn't know that."

"You're the only person at the office who really talks to me. You're the only one who even really looks at me. That exchange we had in the conference room yesterday is the first real conversation I've had with any salesperson in the company ever."

"What about David? He talks to you, doesn't he?"

"That's just business. He never asks about my personal life—and we never do anything social outside of work—not unless everyone else is going, too. We never talk about anything other than the business. He knows literally nothing about me."

"Do you know anything about him?"

She explodes in laughter and her cheeks blush. She makes me weak in the knees when she smiles like that.

"I know everything about him. I run his business and handle his personal finances. There is nothing about that man I don't know—but he likes to blind himself to the fact. He likes to pretend it isn't happening so he can continue to see me as a mindless drone. Occasionally bantering with him doesn't change that."

"Isn't that what we're doing?" I ask. "Aren't we bantering?"

"We're bantering in a social setting with no one else from the company around. I'm asking you questions about your past and you're evading telling me anything."

I can't look at her. "I won't ask you anything about yourself, either."

"You can ask me anything you want. That's why I'm here—because I want us to get to know each other."

"Why?" I ask. "I'm nobody."

"I just told you why and I'm nobody, too. I'm a file clerk in a tiny office in a no-name town in New Jersey. No one cares about me."

I find my eyes riveting to her face. "I care about you."

Her eyelashes dip in the most sensual possible way. "I know you do. That's why I want to get to know you."

I try to break the tension by taking a sip of my coffee. It warms my insides, but it doesn't melt the tension. "You might not like me if you found out anything about me."

"I'll never know if I don't find out. How bad can it be? You don't know me from a hole in the ground. If I find out and I decide I don't want to have anything to do with you, you haven't lost anything."

I find myself studying her. I would definitely lose something if she told me she didn't want to have anything to do with me. I'm not sure if I could handle that.

She's giving me something here—something more than all this attention.

I'm as much of a nobody as she is. I have no money, no future, no name. I'm as much of a nobody as a high school kid washing cars on the corner or flipping burgers in the back of this coffee shop right now.

She actually is interested in me. She wants to know who I am—and not because I'm a bigshot business tycoon from New York with more money than he knows what to do with. She doesn't know anything about that.

She's interested in *me*—the real me. I could tell her anything about myself—anything other than that. She would be interested. That's why she's here. She really is the only person who cares enough even to ask.

None of the other salespeople at the office have asked me a single question about myself—apart from why I left New York and who I worked for before this. None of them wants to know me as a person. Neither does David.

I couldn't sacrifice this priceless gift Vivian is giving me. I just want to sit here and enjoy it while it lasts.

Not telling her anything might spoil the whole thing. She might decide I'm too closed and I'm being dishonest with her.

I'll just have to live with the consequences if that happens. I can't jeopardize my shot to get back on top. I have to stick to my plan and ride it to the end.

She sees me scrutinizing her. "What's on your mind?" she asks. "What are you thinking about?"

"I'm thinking about you. I'm thinking about what a treasure you are and how it is that no one even knows."

"You know," she replies. "It didn't take much for you to find out."

"You're the one who invited me here. I wouldn't have found out if not for you."

She won't stop staring at me. "Maybe you're a treasure, too. I won't know that unless you give me something to work with."

I shrug and look down at my coffee. "I really wish I could."

"What's stopping you? Why the big secret?"

"You wouldn't be interested in me if you knew."

"Isn't that for me to decide? I might still be interested."

"I don't mean like that. You wouldn't be interested in me the same way. You would see me differently."

"I would see you accurately. I can't see you accurately now."

The blood rushes to my cheeks. She understands so much more than I do.

She loses patience with my silence, tosses back the rest of her cocoa, and stands up. "I better go get my car."

"I'll come with you." I stand up, too.

I throw some cash on the table and we leave the coffee shop. I shouldn't waste my money on coffee shop coffee, but I can make an exception for her.

We head up the street to the shop where she gets her keys and pays at the counter. We meet back up on the sidewalk. "Thank you again for last night," she tells me. "You were really kind and considerate."

"Do you remember the welcome letter where you told me I shouldn't hesitate to call on you if I needed anything?"

"Of course I remember," she tells me. "That's what I'm here for."

"Well, I'd like you to think of me the same way. You have my number. Call me if you need anything at all. I mean it. I would really like it if you did."

She blushes again. "You're really sweet. I appreciate it."

"Thank you for inviting me out. It means a lot. It really does. I really value being able to talk to you the way we do even if I can't tell you everything right now."

"Will you ever? If you can't do it right now, does that mean you'll be able to do it later?"

"I hope so. I really do. I hope it will be very soon."

She smiles. "Okay. I can live with that—but I won't promise not to be insatiably curious."

I find myself smiling back at her. "I can live with that. Just don't bet too much money in the pool."

She laughs and heads for her car. "I would never waste my money on that. I'll see you at the office on Monday."

I stand on the sidewalk and watch her reverse out of her parking space before she drives off into town. She glows with so much light and energy. I love everything about being around her—except that I have to keep so many secrets from her.

I wish I could tell her everything. Maybe someday soon I'll be able to. I just hope she still cares enough to listen to me when I tell her.

I hope some other lucky fool doesn't come along and sweep her off her feet before I can do it myself.

Chapter 7: Vivian

I step into the office and immediately sense a pulse of tension running through the place. There shouldn't be any tension in the place because it's first thing Monday morning. None of the salespeople are here yet.

David's car sits in the parking lot outside—and then I hear voices coming from the conference room.

I go to my desk, put away my handbag and hang up my coat, and turn on my computer before David comes out of his office.

"Come on down to the conference room," he tells me. "I need you to be there for this."

"What's going on?" I ask. "Who's in there?"

"The executive board is in there. They're calling an emergency meeting. I need you to sit in as a witness and impartial observer—not to mention recording the meeting for our records."

I gulp. This is serious. The Cast Iron Securities Executive Board never comes down here to visit. David always goes to visit them in their Trenton office when he needs to attend their meetings.

This is an emergency, though. I wonder what it's about.

I grab my tablet and follow David to the conference room. The eight executives are already sitting down at the table—four per side.

The executives greet David on his way into the room. They shake his hand when he heads down to sit in his usual chair at the far end of the table.

I stand next to his shoulder, switch on my tablet, and open my voice recorder app. I'll record the meeting and then transcribe it into text for the company records.

The executives talk amongst themselves, but I only hear them exchanging pleasantries and small talk. They don't discuss anything I would consider an emergency.

None of them acts like this is an emergency, either. They all act perfectly casual and relaxed like they just came down here for the scenery.

I'm just wondering if this wasn't all a giant mistake when the front door of the office opens out in the main room.

The tension in the conference room skyrockets through the roof as we all listen to footsteps coming closer.

My heart stops when Derek walks in and stops by the empty chair at the opposite end of the table. David stays seated when he waves at the chair. "Take a seat, man. We're all grateful you could come in and clear up this matter."

"Clear up what matter?" Derek's eyes dart around the room—to everyone but me. He erases me from existence.

"It has come to our attention that you've been selling securities, financial instruments, and other financial products on the side—apart from what you're selling here at Cast Iron Securities," Sherman Wilfrey cuts in. "We want to hear it from you—because, if you are selling these instruments on the side, that would create a conflict of interest with your employment here."

Derek's hard eyes snap to Sherman's face. "I have been selling them—but if you know all of that, then you know I'm not selling Cast Iron Securities products."

"What are you selling?" David interrupts.

Derek takes a deep breath. I see him gathering himself for a full-scale assault. "I'm selling products for a company called Whirlwind Investment Assets. I can show you the instruments in question and prove to you that they are very different from anything you're selling at Cast Iron Securities."

"Are you selling these other products on company time?" Alistair Fiero asks.

Derek braces himself again. He expects the worst from this. That's the only explanation for his behavior.

"There is no such thing as company time," Derek replies. "My employment with Cast Iron Securities is entirely based on commissions. If I don't sell, I don't get paid and I only get paid for selling Cast Iron Securities products. What I do and how I spend my time each day doesn't figure into it. I'm not using this office, its computer network, its printers, its staff, or any other Cast Iron infrastructure to sell these products—and I can also prove that I'm not courting any of Cast Iron's customers or prospects. Whirlwind is a completely different company with a completely different target clientele in a completely different pricing tier. Whirlwind isn't in competition with Cast Iron at all."

"How would you prove that?" Sherman asks.

"I would show you Whirlwind's products. I can also show you the sales records from all the sales I've closed since I started working here. You'll see that none of the customers are customers of Cast Iron, have never been prospects or leads, and that the pricing and investment classes are in a completely different industry category from Cast Iron's customer base."

Alistair frowns to himself. "I've been in this industry for forty years and I've never heard of Whirlwind before. Where is it located?"

Derek inhales a deep steadying breath. "It's a start-up, actually. I'm just starting this business on my own. I'm funding it with my own money and keeping everything strictly separate from Cast Iron."

Dead silence falls over the table—all except for the sound of jaws hitting the carpet.

David finally gasps. "You're starting your own securities company?! Your own financial instruments company?!"

Derek dips his chin once. "That's right. If you can find any grounds to show that anything I'm doing crosses the two companies, then I'll resign my employment here—but I give you my word of honor that you won't find anything. If you know about this at all, then you know I'm not selling Cast Iron products to anyone other than Cast Iron prospects. Whirlwind prospects aren't interested in Cast Iron products and vice versa."

Sherman rubs his chin. "That is one hell of a story, son."

Derek looks back and forth at everyone. "Is that all you wanted to talk to me about?"

"Um….only that you're doing a great job here," David interrupts. "You're knocking it out of the park and we don't want to lose you."

"You don't have to," Derek replies. "I'm not doing anything wrong. I can send you the information if you really want to see it. I have nothing to hide."

"That would be great," Sherman replies. "We really appreciate you coming in to explain it to us. You can go back to work. I'm sure you have prospects to visit today."

Derek leaves the room. Everyone sits in stunned silence for a minute. "This is incredible!" Sherman breathes. "I don't know if I can believe it."

David puffs out his cheeks. "This is definitely a first. I've never had a salesman start a company of his own on the side—and keep it hidden from everyone."

"What are we going to do?" Alistair asks.

"There is nothing we can do," Sherman replies. "He's right. He isn't doing anything wrong. We can go over his paperwork when he sends it to us, but something tells me he's telling the truth about this. He wouldn't be so forthcoming to show us everything if he didn't already know he was in the right."

"I don't like it," Alistair murmurs. "What if he really is in competition with us? He could put us out of business."

"I don't think so," David replies. "He sounds like knows exactly what he's doing. He sounds like he's been keeping it under his hat that he knows more about this industry than any of us. Now he's putting it into practice and starting his own operation. If he says he isn't in competition with us, I believe him."

"So you're just going to let him continue to build his own company right here from his cubicle desk?" Alistair fires back.

"What's the alternative—fire him? He'll only build his own company somewhere else. The guy is bringing in more money than all the rest of my salespeople combined. I'm not going to fire him when he isn't doing anything wrong. I say more power to him. If he gets his start here, maybe he'll put in a good word for us later. I'm proud of him. I really hope he does it. In fact, I'm sure he will."

Chapter 8: Derek

I come out of the office just as Vivian is getting out of her car. She smirks at me. "Working late again?"

"Or early—one or the other."

"Don't you ever sleep?"

"Not unless I absolutely have to."

She studies me. "How's the new company coming along?"

"It's going well. I'm getting a lot of new customers, so I'm happy with how it's going."

She shakes her head while she locks her car. "I still can't believe you're actually doing this."

"Why is it so surprising? I don't want to be a salesman for the rest of my life."

"You're the first salesman I've met who feels that way."

I spun around to stare at her. "I can't be. Are you telling me none of the others have ambitions—or plans?"

"I wouldn't know about that because they don't discuss their ambitions or plans with me—but I think they would have mentioned it to someone around the water cooler if they did have ambitions or plans. They talk about everything else they do outside of work. I don't think any of them could keep their mouths shut about something like that if they were actually doing it."

Now it's my turn to shake my head. "That's terrible. Everyone should strive to be more than what they are."

"What about me?" she asks. "Should I strive to be more than what I am?"

I feel my cheeks burn. "I wasn't talking about you."

"You said everyone. I'm someone. Therefore what you said applies to me, too."

"*Do* you have ambitions or plans?" I ask. "Do you strive to be more than what you are?"

"No. Do you think less of me because of it?"

I want to look away. "I don't think less of you. I just want to understand why not. You're smart. You're insightful. You're obviously savvy and organized and motivated if you handle this company so well for David. There's no limit to what you could become."

Now she's the one who looks away and turns red. "I doubt it. I'll probably work here for the rest of my life."

"Why?" I ask. "You can't enjoy it so much that everyone ignores you and undervalues you."

"It's a good job. It pays the bills."

"Is that all your life is worth? Don't you ever dream of more? This can't be what you wanted to be when you were little. What was your real dream?"

She turns away. "I don't want to talk about it."

I shoot out my hand to grab her arm. I don't know what made me react like that, but I can't let her walk away with those words hanging between us. "You said you wanted to know about me. I want to know about you."

"You first," she fires back. "Tell me about yourself. Then maybe I'll tell you about me—not before."

She tries to break away again, but I hold her back. I don't give myself a second to hesitate before I dive in and kiss her.

She freezes for a minute before her lips melt in my mouth. Her whole being melts into my arms and she starts kissing me back.

That kiss escalates in a slow, sultry, powerful tide of pure romantic bliss. Her lips taste unbelievably good. I can't get enough.

She's wearing a cherry lip gloss that only adds to the succulent sweet delicacy of her mouth. My tongue glides into her mouth and swirls around her tongue before we both drift apart on a pillow of cloud.

"Go out with me," I breathe into her mouth. "I'll tell you everything if you just go out with me."

Her eyes widen. "Really? You mean....like on a date?"

"Yes, on a date. Dinner.....and whatever happens after that. We can talk. I'll tell you about me and you can tell me about you. I want to know everything. If you knowing everything is the only way I can find out, then I'll do it."

"Yes!" she whispers. "I'll go out with you."

"I'll pick you up tomorrow at seven, okay?"

She nods fast. Her eyes brim with some hidden emotion. It looks like a painful emotion, but it only makes her look even more unfathomably beautiful.

I want to move in and kiss her again. I want to smash her against this car and grind into her until I make her orgasm right here in front of the office.

I'm just about to do exactly that when David's car rolls into the parking lot. I turn away and pretend that Vivian and I were just talking so he doesn't notice anything.

She starts talking to David and they enter the building together. I distinctly hear him ask her where I'm going. I don't hear her answer.

I get into my car and drive back to my apartment. It's an extremely basic studio on the very top floor of an apartment complex downtown. It isn't the nicest place around, but it's cheap.

I can afford something much better, especially with all the bonuses David has been giving me. I don't want to spend my money on that. I channel every spare dollar into my business.

The sooner I get it off the ground, the sooner I'll start making the kind of money that will justify me moving somewhere much nicer.

I have a lot to do, but getting ready for my date with Vivian takes the top priority. I call into the office and tell Vivian to tell David that I'm out with prospects and customers who have already bought from me. That gets me off the hook for the rest of the day.

First, I take my bonus money, drive up to Trenton, and buy a really, really nice suit with all the trimmings. I'm going to need it and I can afford it now.

I pay extra so they'll tailor it for me while I wait.

I'm exhausted from all these late nights, so I drive back to my apartment and crash hard. I don't wake up until a few hours before it's time for me to go pick up Vivian.

I take extra time getting ready. I don't trouble myself much when I go to work at Cast Iron Securities. I want my appearance to blend in with the local habitat.

I go all out and make sure I get every detail perfect. I want to knock her socks off, especially if I'm going to be telling her things about myself that might drive her away for good.

I finish up some tasks on my business while I count down the seconds until it's time to go. I would like to show up at her door in a really nice car, but that would probably be too much for our very first date.

This suit is probably too much for our very first date, but I'm doing it anyway. I don't want to show up looking like a bum—which is what everyone at the office already thinks I am.

I force myself to stay calm when I drive across town to her apartment. She lives on the ground floor of a mid-level apartment complex. I don't know what the apartments are like inside, but the exterior looks a lot better than my building.

I know she makes a decent salary at work, too. It isn't as much as the salespeople make and definitely not as much as they could make if they just put a little more effort into it.

That's the thing about the other salespeople. They care more about rubbing elbows with each other around the water cooler than they do about getting after it and closing sales.

But tonight isn't about that. I walk up to the door and knock. She comes out wearing a knee-length powder blue ruffle dress with puffed sleeves and a ruffled, scrunched top.

I would have expected the blue to contrast unpleasantly with her eyes, but they actually accentuate each other and make her eyes look even brighter.

The dress perfectly hugs her curves. She undulates from side to side when she walks on her tall white heels. Every part of her stands out as the pinnacle of sexiness.

She stops dead in her tracks and stares at me in my suit. I didn't expect to make that much of an impression, but I guess I underestimated what a suit like this can do.

I stop dead in my tracks and stare at her in that dress. She wears her hair up in a messy bun with whisps of brightly tinted curls falling all around her face.

I try to tear my eyes away and my gaze darts to the apartment behind her. It's a simple one-bedroom apartment with no frills at all. I would have expected her to rent a nicer place considering how much she makes, but maybe she has other reasons for staying here. What do I know?

She opens her mouth and closes it a few times. "What is.....*that?*" she chokes.

"This?" I look down. "I got a new suit. I wanted to make a good impression. Do you like it?"

She gulps and looks away. "It's amazing. You look great."

"You look beautiful. Are you ready?"

She takes a white clutch handbag off a side table right inside the door. She steps out, locks the door behind her, and turns to face me.

I lead her to my car, open the passenger door for her, and I cringe when she sits down on the seat. I really wish I could drive her in something nicer. I don't want her to get her dress dirty in my car.

Not that my car is dirty. I just wish it was nicer. I would have liked to take her on a date in a limo, but I'm not there yet.

Chapter 9: Derek

I drive into town and park outside the restaurant where I've made reservations. It isn't the nicest restaurant I could take Vivian to, but I don't want to frighten her with too much too fast. She probably already thinks this is too much.

I lead her inside and she blushes and fights back a grin when we sit down at the table. "So....."

"So," I reply. "Here we are—alone at last."

She snickers. "So spill your guts. Do you have a basement full of dead bodies?"

I laugh. It's the first time I can remember laughing since I left New York. I didn't want to laugh, but her presence makes me want to do it now.

"What's the pool up to?" I ask. "How much are they putting on the axe-murdering psychopath theory?"

Her eyes dart away. "I'm sure I don't know. I don't keep track of that."

My eyebrows shoot up. "You don't? I thought you were keeping an eye on things to find out which story turned out to be the right one."

"I keep track of the different options and storylines people come up with. I don't keep track of the odds or how much everyone is betting on each one. I don't have time for that."

I laugh again. "Good idea. I don't have time for it, either, and I'm the one they're betting on. Any of them could find out if they just came right out and asked me."

"Would you tell them? I've been asking you all this time and you haven't told me yet."

I pretend to straighten my napkin. "That's true."

"You said you would tell me if I went out with you. Well, here we are. I'm out with you."

I open my mouth to say something, but right then, the waiter comes over with water, bread and butter, and our menus. He asks if we want to order any drinks. I order a bottle of wine for both of us and ask her if she wants anything. She doesn't.

I find myself squirming in my chair after he leaves.

She doesn't let me off the hook at all. "Okay, we really are alone now. You were saying?"

I open my mouth, but right at that moment, someone comes up to our table. It isn't a member of the restaurant staff.

The guy's name is Brody Ketterman. He's a reporter who works in New York. Don't ask me what he's doing all the way down here in Jersey.

He walks right up to the table and sticks his hand out. "Mr. Salazar—it's so good to see you again! Do you remember me? I interviewed you for *Business Weekly* last year. How are you?"

I shake his hand. "I'm fine. Thank you. Yes, I remember you."

"Are you down here on business? Hey, would you be willing to do another interview? I know my readers would love it if I did a follow-up piece on the Apico Acquisitions takeover of Titanium Finance. Everyone is in stitches to find out what happened to you after you left New York. Do you have any plans to make a comeback? We would love to know what you're doing."

My scalp prickles when I feel Vivian watching this. "I'm in the middle of something here," I tell him. "Contact me at a more appropriate time."

His gaze darts to Vivian like he's just seeing her for the first time. A woman this stunning can't be so invisible to everyone. I can't be the only man in the room who notices what a knockout she is.

His expression changes in a fraction of an instant. "Oh...okay. Sorry," he stammers. "I'll see you later..."

He hustles away. Now I have to deal with Vivian staring at me with her eyes bugging out of their sockets. "What....the hell.....was that about?" she husks. "You.....you were on the cover of *Business Weekly?!*"

I try to lower my eyes to the tablecloth, but I wind up holding her gaze. "I didn't want anyone to find out, but I guess it's going to come out anyway."

"You....." She clamps her eyes shut. "You were involved with the Apico Acquisitions takeover of Titanium Finance?!"

"I was more than involved. I built Titanium Finance. It was my company. I was on top of the world before the takeover."

"What do you mean—you built it?!" she gasps. "You mean....."

"I started it in my college dorm room. I built it into the multi-billion-dollar business that it is now. Apico wouldn't have looked sideways at Titanium if not for me." I find myself looking out at the restaurant. "Now I'm here."

"But.....you would have gotten a huge payout from the takeover! You would have gotten enough to start something else."

I snort. "That wasn't how it happened at all. They wanted to keep me on as a consultant or another executive. I would have been a trophy on the wall. I wasn't going to do that in my own company. So I left."

"You left.....with nothing?!"

"Can you blame me? I wasn't going to stick around and become an employee in my own business. I would rather put my efforts into starting something else—something that's completely mine. I won't take Whirlwind public. It will always stay private so that never happens again."

"But.....how will you raise capital?! How will you ever get that big if you never go public?"

I shrug. "That isn't as important as staying independent and making sure I'm always the one in charge of my own company. No one will ever carry out a hostile takeover on me again."

She gapes at me in horrified shock—and then gulps. She squeezes her eyes tight shut again. "That's why you were talking to Jackson Metcalfe and Dante Helme, isn't it? You know them."

"I was in The Billionaires' Club—once upon a time. I'm not anymore." I take a deep breath. "And now you know. I understand if you aren't interested in me because of it. That's what I liked the most about you. You didn't know and you were still interested in me. You never knew or cared that I once had money."

"I am still interested in you!" she exclaims. "I'm more interested in you! Did you really think I would walk away because of that?"

"I wasn't sure. I didn't want to take the chance—and I didn't want you to like me because of that."

"I don't," she insists. "Stop saying that."

"Okay," I murmur. "I won't say it anymore."

She stares at me in stunned silence for a few more minutes. Her scrutiny is really making me uncomfortable.

I wait while the waiter delivers our bottle of wine. Then I lean forward. "So now you know about me. What's going on with you?"

"What do you mean?"

"You said you would explain to me why you're working as an admin clerk and why you have no ambitions or goals to do anything else."

She looks away and she doesn't look back. I want her attention back on me, so I pick up her hand and hold it across the table.

She still won't look at me. "You know the truth about me," I murmur. "This is what you wanted. You said you wanted us to know each other. What would that mean if not you telling me about yourself? Do you really think I'm going to stop being interested in you if I find out?"

She yanks her hand out of my grasp, sticks both hands into her lap, squares her shoulders, and throws back her head. "I take care of my mother. That's the truth. Most of my pay goes toward covering her rent, bills, food, medical costs—all of that. That's why I don't have any ambitions. I have a good job that takes care of both of us. I don't want anything to jeopardize that. She won't be around forever. Then I'll think about doing something else, but not until then. For right now, I just need to keep my head down, bring home a paycheck, and not thinking about anything else."

I frown at her. "That's it? Why did you think you had to hide that?"

"You made a big deal about me not having ambitions. You made a big deal about what I wanted to be when I was young. I don't have the luxury of thinking that way. You might be able to walk away with nothing, but I couldn't."

"I'm not saying you have to walk away with nothing. I'm not even saying you have to stop working for Cast Iron Securities. Hell, *I* work for Cast Iron Securities. I work there full time and take home a paycheck while I build my dreams on the side."

She frowns at me. "Really?"

"Of course. What did you think—that you would have to quit your job and starve in the streets to make your dream come true?"

"Yes," she replies. "That's what everyone says."

I shake my head and pull the cork out of the wine bottle. "It doesn't work that way. Very few people have the luxury of doing it that way. Most have to get a regular job—sometimes a job that they hate. Some already have families to support or other obligations. You work on your dream on the side when you have the free time. You asked me why I don't sleep very much. That's why. I have no choice but to dedicate a certain amount of time and effort to my job. I want to maximize the rest of my time toward my dream. That's the way you do it."

She furrows her brow in thought. "I never thought of it that way before."

"What would you be doing if you could do it that way?"

"I don't know. I never thought about that, either."

"Well, what were you interested in when you were younger—before you started taking care of your mother?"

"Well.....I really liked cooking....and gardening.....I grew up in a rural part of Pennsylvania. My family had a big property with a bunch of acres and livestock and a huge garden. My mom grew most of our food in the garden and we used to get cows butchered every year of our meat. I really liked helping out with that. I liked canning the food and then coming up with creative ways to cook with it."

Now I'm the one who winds up staring at her. "Really? That sounds amazing."

She makes a face at me. "You only think that because you grew up selling comic books on the streets of South Philly. It was normal to me."

"I can't imagine doing something like that. It sounds like some kind of paradise."

She beams at me. "It was. It was a beautiful way to live and a beautiful way to grow up. If I was going to do something like that, I would like to share that kind of thing with the world. I always wind up watching cooking shows on YouTube. Some of those women have their own kitchen gardens and some even raise their own chickens and rabbits and stuff for meat."

"Wow," I exclaim. "That is so far out of my world."

She laughs at me. "It's just a pipe dream. I would never be able to afford a property big enough to do something like that."

"You could start a YouTube cooking channel of your own. You could easily do that on the side while you're working at Cast Iron Securities."

She bursts out laughing, blushes, and covers her mouth to stifle the noise. "No, I couldn't! Me—on YouTube?! You're crazy!"

"Why? You're gorgeous. You obviously have a talent and a passion for this. Why not? Do you get creative when you cook for yourself at home?"

"No way! I don't need to. It's just me. I can just stick the food in the microwave and dump it down my throat."

Now it's my turn to laugh. "I'm not sure I want to get involved in that."

She won't stop blushing. "I could never go on YouTube. I would die of embarrassment."

"You only say that because you've never done it before. Imagine if your channel blew up and you had a few million people tuning in to watch your videos every week. Imagine they were writing comments back and forth and learning something from it."

She waves that away. "That would never happen."

"Imagine there's someone out there like me who has never done anything like that before, but they have the same dream of living a country lifestyle. Who are they supposed to learn from if they don't learn from you?"

"There are plenty of other content creators out there doing the same thing. The person could learn from any of them. They wouldn't learn anything new from me."

"But they wouldn't learn your unique perspective on it. They wouldn't get your passion and your love for the process. You might be able to speak to those people in ways no one else can. Your personality and your unique perspective on it might inspire someone in ways they don't get from anyone else."

She turns around and leans forward to rest her elbow on the table. "Is that what you do? Do you try to inspire people with your unique perspective on financial instruments and securities portfolios?"

She probably means it as a joke, but I let it slide. "I use my unique perspective in my sales presentations. I use my unique perspective to craft products that are unlike anything else on the market. I fill a need by being unique. No one on the market can give my customers what I give them. That's why they buy from me. It's up to me to make them understand what I'm offering and to show them that they can't get it anywhere else."

She looks away. "I couldn't do something like that."

"Just think about it. Think about ways you could stretch yourself and start having a life outside of work."

"Why should I?" she asks. "I don't need it. I have a good job. It's enough for what I need. I don't need anything else."

I cock my head to study her. "Is that really true?"

"Of course it's true. Why wouldn't it be? I've been working at Cast Iron for years. I don't need anything else."

I point at her. "I don't believe you. You said earlier that you would wait until your mother wasn't around anymore before you think about pursuing your dreams. That means you do have dreams and ambitions. You already know you're dissatisfied with your job because you know it isn't what you really want to do—but I just proved to you that you could pursue your dreams right now without compromising your income or your mother or your job."

She shakes her head and looks away. "I can't think about it right now. I just have to keep doing what I'm doing and not think about anything else."

The waiter comes back just then to take our orders, so I let the subject drop. I don't stop thinking about it, though.

There's so much more to Vivian than I realized. What a good person she is for taking care of her mother.

I actually understand why she feels like she can't think about anything else. It must be really hard for her. She could have a much better life if she spent her pay on herself instead of her mother.

Vivian must realize how badly she's cramping her own life. She's sacrificing so much more than money—and she does it so she can do the right thing for someone in need—someone she loves.

That means the world to me. It makes me value her so much more than I did before. She has a beautiful heart—even more beautiful than I realized.

I make up my mind then and there not to bring up the subject of her dreams and ambitions again. She isn't ready for that. If she does it, she does it. If she doesn't, she doesn't.

The reason she doesn't do it makes her so much more of a treasure than if she did do it. I respect her decision too much to argue with her or pressure her.

I sure wish I could take the weight off her shoulders. I wish I could free her from this burden so she could pursue something she's really passionate about. I wish I could make it so she didn't have to worry about money anymore.

She probably isn't ready for that—and neither am I. She probably wouldn't appreciate me trying to take the responsibility away from her. She doesn't sound like she wants to change anything about the way she's doing things. I can respect that.

I take a chance and extend my hand across the table. I leave it lying there in front of her.

She looks down at it and then places her hand in mine without looking up at me.

"I'm sorry if I made you uncomfortable," I tell her. "I won't bring it up again."

She shakes her hair out of her eyes and looks away at the other diners. "Let's talk about something else. How long did you live in New York?"

"Fifteen years. I went there straight after college. I was there right up until the Apico takeover."

"And.....you were a billionaire....and everything....."

"I'm not that person anymore."

She shoots a sidelong look at my suit. "I'd say you are. You've been in hiding down here."

"Does that bother you?"

"I just can't imagine living like that. It's a different world."

"It's the same world. All the people there are just people. They all put their pants on one leg at a time. They all get sick in the winter and get their clothes dirty when they wear them. Things like that don't change just because you have money."

"And you want to get back to that? You want to get that kind of money again?"

"It isn't about the money. It's about all the things we just talking about. It's about being the best version of myself, doing a job I'm passionate about, and making a positive difference in other people's lives. It's about never settling for what the world dishes out and always striving for something greater. The outcome isn't as important as the process."

"Are you saying you're enjoying the process of working a full-time job you don't like, putting in all these hours on the side, and driving a secondhand car? Do you love that part of the process?"

"I'm dissatisfied with where I am right now, but I do love the process of working to improve my situation. I wouldn't be satisfied with just accepting my fate as a low-level salesman in someone else's company. I'm not cut out for that." She looks away and I try to get her attention by squeezing her hand. "We said we weren't going to talk about that. Tell me more about the way you grew up. Why did you move to New Jersey?"

"I went to Penn State for college. I was still there when my dad seven years ago. My mom had health problems and couldn't keep up the farm by herself, so I left school, got this job, and moved her down here."

"Wouldn't it cost less if you both lived in the same apartment? Paying rent on two places must cost a fortune."

She grimaces and rolls her eyes to heaven. "I tried that. Believe me. Us living in the same apartment does NOT work. Trust me."

"Why not? What's wrong with it?"

"It just doesn't. I need my own space where I can get away from her and where I only see her when I'm ready to see her. When we lived in the same apartment, she would just randomly come out of her room, sit down next to me on the couch, and start talking to me about everything on her mind. She would want to talk to me about what I was watching on the computer or what I was making for dinner or what my work schedule was going to be that week. She drove me insane because I couldn't get away from her. If I was slouching on the couch watching cooking videos, she would want to watch and talk to me about them when I just wanted to turn my brain off and not deal with anyone. It works much better like this where we each have our own space."

"How often do you see her?"

"Three or four times a week. I take her groceries over there, we make dinner together, and spend the evening just hanging out doing whatever and talking. It's really nice. I can enjoy it because I know that, at the end of the evening, I'm going to go home to my own place where I can do what I want without discussing it with her. I need a certain amount of real estate in my mind that is mine. I couldn't have that with her around."

"Did you explain to her that you needed your own personal space?"

"I couldn't tell her that. She's my mother. I could have gone into my bedroom and watched videos while I was lying on my bed with the door shut. She wouldn't have bothered me then, but she would have thought I was pushing her away. I didn't want her to feel like she was unwelcome. I just wanted her to keep to her own space and leave me in mine."

"How did she feel when you moved her out and got her a separate space?"

"She was fine with it. I explained that I needed to have my own place to myself and it wasn't because I didn't love her. I told her we would still see each other all the time and she said she kind of preferred to have her own place, too. So it worked out in the end."

Chapter 10: Vivian

Derek parks his car outside my apartment, opens my door for me, and slips his hand into mine on our way up to the front door.

He pulls me to a stop on the doorstep. "I'm really glad we talked the way we did tonight. I'm glad we both got our cards out on the table. I feel better."

"Me, too," I tell him. "I don't want us to have any more secrets from each other."

He stares deeply into my eyes. "That's what I want, too."

I squeeze his hand. "I guess this is good night."

"Yeah," he breathes. "Can I kiss you right now?"

My cheeks flush. "If you absolutely have to."

He grins. "I absolutely have to."

He eases in and kisses me gently. His lips soften and warm my face. His hands slip around my cheeks and he pulls me deeper into his mouth.

He kisses slowly, romantically. He doesn't push it any further. I relax into it. I don't expect it to go any further, but it sure feels nice, now that it's happening.

I wrap my arms around his neck and his arms circle my waist. I'm still wearing my heavy winter coat. He can't feel anything back there, but the coat falls open in the front. My body touches his.

My dress is so much thinner than his suit. His suit feels cold through the thin fabric, but I would have to be dead not to feel the tension building in him.

His body feels powerful and explosive in this suit. The suit gives him confidence and mastery he never shows at work.

He pulls me tighter against him and my breath catches when I feel him escalating. He doesn't change the pressure of his lips at all, but the energy radiating through him blows me out of the water.

He leans just a little farther forward and arches my back. I have to hold onto him tighter while the passion and intensity of his kiss builds to a breaking point. I have to struggle to keep up with him.

That energy floods me and turns me on in a rush of blistering desire. Without warning, all that heat rushes to his crotch and he grinds it into me standing right there on the doorstep.

That feeling excites me out of my mind. I can't take this anymore. I need him. I need to lose control with him even if it's just for one night.

I didn't tell him the truth about what my life has really been like since I've been taking care of my mother. I haven't been with a man in all that time. My body is going crazy.

He has to be the one. I want him. I want to let my guard down with him and let all that pent-up frustration out in one night of unbridled passion.

He seems to be thinking the same thing. As soon as it starts, the dam breaks and neither of us tries to hold it back anymore. I gasp for air and ripple my body down his so I can feel how raging hard he's getting.

He responds by flexing his knees and grinding deeper between my legs.

Lightning quick, he pushes me back against the apartment door. He pins me so fast that he takes my breath away.

In seconds, he's working his hips between my legs, scooping his hands down to my ass, and lifting my thighs around him so he can tease me to the stars.

I moan and whine as the passion and energy builds between us. Does he realize how aching wet he makes me? I could climax right here just from the pressure of his crotch between my legs.

He devours my mouth, mauls down my neck, and makes me yelp when he nibbles my breasts through my dress. He pulls my thighs on either side of his hips and lifts my feet off the floor so he can drive me farther up the door and attack my chest.

My fingers trace through his hair, but I don't want to do it with him like this. I have to take him inside my apartment.

I fight my way out of his grasp, turn around, and try to get my keys out of my purse. He attacks me from behind, bites my neck and ears, and drills his rock-hard package into my ass.

He won't stop clawing his fingertips up my thighs. He scoops his hands between my legs, pulls my legs apart, and eventually gets under my dress until both his hands slide up to my panties.

I whine and almost scream out when he dives his fingers inside my panties and starts rubbing and fingering me to the ends of the earth. I can barely concentrate on getting out my keys and trying to unlock the door.

I try to put the key into the lock, but right at that moment, he plunges his fingers into me and sends me reeling into an unbelievable orgasm unlike anything I've ever experienced.

I gasp and start to scream. He clamps his hand over my mouth from behind and pulls my head back onto his shoulder so he can rasp in my ear.

He keeps pumping his fingers into me deeper and harder than I can stand. I can't stop spiking into one mind-blowing orgasm after another. I can't stop as long as he's holding me like this.

"Oh, yeah! Oh, yeah!" he rasps in my ear. "That's so good! You want that so bad, don't you? Come on. You are so damn sweet, baby. I can't wait to get my hands on your sweet body."

He holds me down so hard and his hand over my mouth gives me permission to let go the way I need to.

I slip into a fantasy of him as the kidnapping axe murderer who will take me home to his basement prison to do whatever he wants to me.

The fantasy triggers something in me. It releases so many desires I never knew I had—desires too perverse to ever see the light of day.

I can let them all out in this moment where we're playing out this fantasy in real life. I struggle against all the torrential explosions going off in me right now. I can't contain them all and I don't have to. He'll contain them for me.

He flattens his weight against me even harder to stop me from struggling. I can scream out as much as I want as long as he silences me like this. The neighbors will never hear.

I push back against the door trying to do something to gain some control over myself and my world.

I completely forget about unlocking the door until he takes his hand out of my panties, turns the key, and the door falls open in front of me.

He's holding me down so tightly that I lose my balance. I can't hold myself up and we both fall forward into the apartment.

We fall face downward with him on top of me from behind. I would fall flat on my face and probably hurt myself, but he breaks my fall and guides both of us down flat on the carpet.

He lands on top of me from behind and attacks me so much harder and more intensely. He keeps his hand over my mouth, pulls up my dress, and tears open his pants before I realize what he's doing.

I freak out when I feel his naked shaft right against my ass. All his weight pins me down—and then he stops. He doesn't go any further.

"Do you want this?" he breathes in my ear. "Do you want me to give it to you right now and make you scream for me? Is that what you want?"

I nod fast. I can't stop moaning in an agony of desire. I've never needed anything as much as this.

He made me orgasm harder than I ever have in my life. I need more of that. I don't want it to end so soon—not when I need him so much.

He rocks his body down mine and grinds his prick into my ass cheeks. He widens his legs and straddles his knees on either side of my thighs so I can't spread my legs.

"Yeah, baby!" he husks. "Oh, yeah! Do you know how many nights I dreamed of this? You are all mine. I am going to take you to the stars."

I can only moan in answer. I know he's going to take me to the stars because he did it just now.

I need him inside me so bad. He knows how dripping wet I am for him. He knows I can't get through tonight without fully satisfying myself on his body.

He keeps working his shaft up and down between my ass cheeks. That movement speaks of so many wicked, untamed, unspoken fantasies I never let myself imagine before. I want them all. I want him to take me in every forbidden way starting right now.

He eventually arches back and drives far enough down to touch his molten shaft to my enflamed slit. I can't take it anymore. He excites me more than I can stand.

He doesn't drill into me and plow me to smithereens the way I expect him to—the way I really need him to.

He stops there still holding me in an iron grip. He screws his hips in circles to rotate the head of his shaft in my wetness.

"Oh, baby!" he croaks. "You want it so damn bad, don't you? You're mine, aren't you? You want me in there. You can't live without me, can you?"

I sob in excruciating need. He must know how much I need this. I can't take the anticipation any longer, but he doesn't finish me off—not like that.

He crams his other hand down between my legs, into my panties, and starts fingering me again. He flattens his fingers on my clitoris and circles in maddening, endless rings that drive me wild.

I howl into his hand. He frees me to make as much noise as I need to as long as he covers my mouth.

His hand pulls my head back right against his ear. His hot breath stabs into my brain saying all the filthy words I need to hear him say.

"You're going to cum for me, baby," he half-whispers. "You're never going to stop cumming for me. This body is all mine. I'm going to make you scream and beg for me. I'm going to infect your mind so you never forget me. You're going to ache for me and me alone. That's right. You need that so bad, don't you? You need to feel how much you want me."

I can't hold back. His fingers turn me on and those words trigger another automatic response. I explode in another brutal orgasm that leaves me thrashing and convulsing in his arms.

"Yeah, baby!" he snarls. "Oh, yeah. That's mine. This is all mine. Cum for me. That's right. Show me how much you want me."

I can't stop. I shove my ass back into him just praying to God I can get him inside before I lose my mind completely.

He still doesn't do it, though. He just stays there, right outside my entrance. He puts just enough pressure on me to tease me to my breaking point. I can't take this.

He brings me to one crushing orgasm after another and still doesn't release me. My screams turn to sobs. How much more can I take?

I'm just about to lose all hope when he screws his rock-hard prick just a little tighter in....and a little more.

I freeze when I feel him about to do it. He keeps fingering me and rubbing me, but that pressure distracts me—and then it melts me as he glides in.

He only enters a few inches before he starts rocking back and forth again. He strokes in tiny, mind-destroying waves that spike my desire into the stratosphere. He doesn't go all the way in. He makes me want it so much more.

I try to throw myself back against him, but I can't move like this. He holds my legs together to increase the sensation and pressure beyond my wildest dreams.

This feels so erotic and powerful. I completely surrender to his hands as he builds up speed and power. He strokes deeper and harder with every thrust while his fingers keep spiraling me out of this world.

He eventually drives all the way in and I crumble in a sea of heavenly rapture. He keeps doing the same thing over and over and over to make me climax again and again exactly the way he said he would.

He consumes my body and I release every ounce of control I ever thought I had. I can't do anything more.

Chapter 11: Derek

I roll off Vivian and she collapses whimpering, sobbing, and disheveled on the floor. She looks so pathetic and broken like this with her dress all crumpled and hitched up around her ass.

Just for a second, I flash back to my fantasy about kidnapping her and taking her home. We're playing out that fantasy now—or we just did.

I know she wanted it and I know she enjoyed it. Now she lies face down and sex-stained on the carpet of her own living room.

Seeing her like this completes the fantasy, but that isn't what I want with her. I kick the front door shut, scoop her up in my arms, and carry her into her bedroom. Now I have to take care of her.

She falls apart on my shoulder, buries her face in my neck, and bursts into tears. Is she crying because she thinks I did wrong by her? It better not be that.

Maybe she's just emotional.

I lay her on the bedspread and get busy taking her clothes off. She lies there sobbing while I tug off her coat, lift her dress over her head, and then peel off her saturated panties and unclip her bra.

I see more than I ever want to see of her milky white thighs, her voluptuous breasts, and every other juicy piece of her.

I want to get my hands on her. Doing it with her like this doesn't satisfy me. I want more—a lot more.

I have to take care of her right now, though. Nothing else matters.

I pull down the covers, tuck her in, and then take my clothes off to climb into bed with her. She didn't invite me to, but I know she needs me to.

I crawl in behind her, wrap my arms around her, and pull her warm, sultry body against me. Holy mother-loving crap, she feels so good!

I bury my face in her neck and hold her. "You are so beautiful, baby," I whisper into her ear. "You are a dream come true. Thank you for what you just did. You gave me such a gift tonight."

She sniffles to herself and hugs my arms closer around her stomach. She doesn't try to talk to me. She just cuddles back against me. Her body warms me and excites me all at the same time, but I won't push her to do it again.

She stops crying after a while. She doesn't pull out of my arms when she grabs a tissue from the night table and blows her nose. Then she settles back in.

"Did I hurt you, baby?" I whisper in her ear. "Did I cross a line you didn't want me to cross?"

"No," she husks under her breath. "It's just been a long time. I....I didn't know I could still do that."

"You're magnificent." I kiss her neck. "You have no idea how sexy you are."

She doesn't speak to answer. She responds in a way I never thought possible.

She winds her ass back against my hips and positions her soaking wet slit directly over my crotch. She takes hold of my hands and puts them directly onto her breasts with no warm-up at all.

I can't believe it when she spirals her hips down on top of me and starts grinding her ass into me to turn me on all over again.

Her back arches and her hips flare when she spreads her thighs. Her magnificent, heart-shaped ass revolves on top of me. I can't stop myself from getting hard, and when I do, she pushes straight back onto me. Holy crap, she really does want this!

Her pendulous globe breasts fall into my hands. I have no choice but to play with them, massage them, and squeeze them.

She moans again and arches into my hands and body. Her wet, swollen channel swallows me in more goodness than I felt in the living room just now.

She escalates so much faster than I do. She pushes up on her hands to get the right angle. Her waist tapers to a perfect hourglass in front of me.

She looks so unbelievably hot like this. I have to take her all the way.

I don't think about it or give myself a chance to doubt. I rotate onto my knees and pull her onto all fours.

She accepts it easily. She does more than accept it. She moans in luscious desire and then throws her head back when I start to nail her nice and deep and hard.

She doesn't scream out of control the way she did before. She turns her head, bares her teeth, and snarls in animal passion. Her breasts bounce with each of my thrusts. She looks so erotic like this that I find myself pounding her harder than I mean to.

I slid my hand up her spine and take hold of her by the back of the neck, but she doesn't seem to mind. In fact, she leans into it and gasps out in pleasure as she takes every brutal stroke.

Her ass spanks my hips and her inner muscles clench when I plow into the deepest corners of her being. She gasps again and again through ragged, panting lips. I can't remember seeing anything as hot as this.

Seeing her drives me over the edge before I can stop myself. I explode inside her and collapse on top of her the way we were before. We're naked now and in her bed. I barely stay conscious enough to roll off her and wrap my arms around her before I drift off into a deep sleep.

I wake up in darkness. I have to take a second to remember where I am. I don't recognize the smell—until I smell Vivian's perfume. I'm in her bed, but she isn't here.

A streetlight casts a silver glow over the room. I'm alone in her apartment. What happened to her?

I roll onto my back and stare at the ceiling feeling the bliss and cosmic relaxation of last night drift over me. She's immaculate. I want her again. Just thinking about her makes me start to get hard, but it's more than that.

Her heart is so pure. She gives herself to me so beautifully. I treasure that about her.

I'm still lying here thinking about her when a door opens somewhere in the apartment. A light shines into the hallway and then switches off.

She slips into the bedroom still naked from before. The streetlight glows on her breasts, hips, and thighs. Mmm. Delicious.

She smiles when she sees me awake. "I didn't mean to wake you up."

"I didn't know where you went." I hold out my hand. "Come here."

She starts to climb between the sheets, but I pull her on top of me instead. I kiss her again while she straddles me and then I push her to sit her up.

She rocks on me and smiles when she feels me getting hard. She angles her hips to take me inside.

I follow her curves, squeeze her breasts to make her moan, and circle her hips to rock her on my shaft.

She smiles down at me in between drifting off in rapture each time I thrust into her.

This feels so much more sensual and connected than what we did before. I ride in a sea of bliss. I don't need to shatter her or do anything else. This feels so good. I don't want to change it.

She touches my chest and then braces her arms against me to pump her hips harder. That position makes her breasts stick out at me. I flick her nipples and savor the delicious moans of excruciating agony that tighten in my guts.

I still want to ravage her. I want to consume her and conquer her, but I can do all of that and feel this, too. All those possibilities exist within her.

She can be my filthy kidnapping victim or my angelic goddess from one minute to the next. She's all those things and more.

"We have to go to work soon," she murmurs.

"I know," I tell her. "I know what I'm going to be thinking about at work today when I see you across the office."

She giggles, but she never stops riding me into the sunset. "What are you going to be thinking about?"

"Bending you over the desk and making you scream in front of everyone. I'm going to be thinking about taking you into the bathroom and driving you up the wall until your moans echo through the building. I'm going to be thinking about taking you out to the car, tilting you back on the seat, pulling your skirt up, and eating you out until you gush all over my face."

She giggles again. "Do you want to know what I'll be thinking about at work today?"

I turn bright red. "I don't know. *Do* I want to know what you'll be thinking about at work today?"

She won't stop grinning at me, but her smile slips when her cheeks flush and she starts rocking faster.

"I'll be thinking about.......crawling under your desk.....and sucking you until you grab me by the hair...." she pants.

I gulp. She is not going there.

She moans out loud and drives her hips back down on me even harder. "I'll be thinking about......unzipping you in the hall and stroking you hard......until you push me against the wall and take me from behind.......I'll be thinking about you lifting my leg over your shoulder while you look into my eyes and finger me until I cum....."

She moans out in deepest longing and her eyes roll back in her skull when she says it. Oh, my God! I need this woman like some kind of drug.

I can think about doing all of those things to her. I want to do all of those things to her. I think about doing a million other wicked, torturous things that all end with both of us roaring in ecstasy and dripping with sweat.

I can't keep lying here anymore. I rear off the bed, flip her onto her back, and arch into her while I watch the interplay of emotions and blissful delirium sweeping over her face.

She moans, rocks, and spasms every time I thrust into her. She's beyond succulent, fragrant, and delectable.

I lean back, take hold of her hips, and pull her into my thrusts while she lies back with her arms above her head. Her majestic body spreads before me, so beautiful, so ripe, so passionate and responsive.

I watch myself taking her to the stars. She moans in deepest fulfillment when I stuff her full of my being. She wants everything I have to give her and I'll never stop until I give her all of it.

Chapter 12: Derek

I slip out of bed so I don't wake up Vivian, but she rouses anyway. She moans and turns over before she looks up and sees me putting my clothes on.

"I have to go home, take a shower, and change before work." I bend over to kiss her. "I'll see you in a few hours."

She groans and buries her face in the pillow. "You did not keep me up all night and now you're running out all bright-eyed and bushy-tailed."

I laugh in spite of myself. "You kept me up all night, too, remember? You aren't going to blame this on me."

She humphs. "Fine. Be that way."

I kiss her again. "I'll see you in two hours—and don't start making eyes at me across the office. It's going to be hard enough working in the same building with you and not ripping your clothes off every time you bend over your filing cabinet."

I slip out of the apartment while she's still in bed. I have to hurry to make it home in time, shower, and change into my regular suit. I don't want to show up in my new one. It's too good for Cast Iron Securities.

I go about my business. I'm already leaving the office to go see my first prospects by the time Vivian comes to work.

I don't see her for the rest of the day until I return to the office. I have a full day of sales to log, so I'm still sitting at my desk when she leaves.

She has to walk past my cubicle to get to the door. She stops there and smiles at me. "Are you going to be working late tonight?"

"No, I'm almost done here."

She blushes. "Do you want to go out for a drink or something after this?"

I look up at her. I don't even have to ask what she means.

We did it last night. We did it multiple times throughout the night, but what does that really mean? Does it mean anything? Does it mean nothing?

I should find out—and what better place to broach the subject than over a drink after work? We don't have to go back to her place right away. We can discuss it first.

"That would be nice," I tell her. "I'll call you as soon as I finish here."

She smiles. "Okay. See you later."

She leaves and I concentrate on my computer screen. I immerse myself in work so I finish quicker.

I don't look up from my computer and my paperwork for another hour before I finish. When I do, I stand up and notice the light still on in David's office. I'm not the only one burning the midnight oil.

I have to give him some of my paperwork anyway, so I finish powering down my computer, pack up my stuff, file everything I need to file, and take the paperwork in there to put it on his desk.

"Hey, man," I tell him. "I brought you those client satisfaction reports you asked for."

I wave the stack at him and slap it down on the desk in front of him. He doesn't look up from his computer.

"Why won't this square up?" he mutters under his breath. "This can't be right. It just won't square up."

I open my mouth to ask what he means and to tell him I'm leaving. He'll be the only one left in the building after this, so he'll have to lock up.

That's when I notice his face dripping with sweat. He looks pale and sweat shines in his hair.

I frown at him. He hasn't looked at me once since I walked in. This isn't like him.

"Are you okay, man?" I ask.

He still doesn't look up. Does he even know I'm here? "Why won't these numbers square up?" he mumbles. "Something must be wrong with this. They won't square no matter what I do."

I'm still studying him in confusion when he raises one hand from the keyboard and rubs the middle of his chest. He flexes his fingers when he does it in an unconscious clawing motion and he winces at the same time.

He compresses his lips just as fast and goes back to what he's doing, but that one movement tells me all I need to know. Something is seriously wrong and it has nothing to do with numbers on a computer screen.

I walk around the desk to his chair to pull him away from the computer. "You gotta come with me, man," I tell him. "I'm taking you to the hospital."

He finally looks up at me. "Huh? What are you talking about?"

"There's something wrong with you. You're having chest pains, aren't you?"

Now he's the one who frowns. He scowls into space. "Oh, yeah. I didn't notice until now."

I take hold of his arm. "Come on. Whatever you're dealing with can wait. We'll take my car in case something goes wrong."

He starts to stand up and then stops to frown at me again. "What do you mean? What are you talking about?"

I can't waste any more time explaining it to him. He must be already suffering from lack of oxygen to the brain.

I pull him the rest of the way to his feet. I keep my hand on his arm to steer him out of the office. I don't trust him even to get that far.

He proves me right when he takes one step and collapses right in front of me. His knees give out and he topples full length on the floor.

I pounce on top of him and grab his shoulders to roll him over. "David!" I yell. "DAVID!!"

He doesn't respond. He's out cold. This is bad.

I scramble to pull out my phone and check his pulse and breathing while I call 911. I don't find a pulse.

I switch the phone to speaker and start doing compressions until a female operator comes on the line.

"911 emergency operator," she chirps. "Please state the nature of the emergency."

"My boss just had a heart attack in front of me!" I gasp. "I'm doing compressions on the floor of his office. He isn't breathing and he doesn't have a pulse! We need an ambulance right away!"

"I'm dispatching EMS personnel now, Sir. Please continue compressions."

"I am!" I pant and have to stop talking so I can breathe into his nose and mouth. Then I go back to doing compressions.

"Does your employer have a history of heart disease?" the operator asks.

"I have no idea!" I gasp. "He seemed healthy until right now."

"Please stay on the line until EMS units arrive."

I'm working too hard to talk. I just concentrate on continuing CPR until the paramedics flood the room.

I buckle into a corner soaking in sweat and totally exhausted by the time they take over. They defibrillate him and get his heart beating again before they wheel him away.

I have to give a report to the Police. They congratulate me on probably saving David's life.

I want to make sure he's all right, so I wait until I can actually stand up again before I get in my car and follow the ambulance to the hospital.

I go inside and find out he's getting his heart catheterized—or he's about to. He's in a waiting room before they take him in for the procedure.

I tell the charge nurse that I'm the one who found him and did CPR on him before the ambulance brought him in. She lets me go back to see him before they take him in for the procedure.

He sinks back onto the pillow when he sees me. "Thank you, man," he croaks. "I owe you big time for this."

"Stop it. I'm just glad you came through it."

He looks up at me. "I need you to check the files on my computer. There's something wrong with them."

My scalp prickles. "You were talking about that when I found you."

"The numbers we sent in for the last five months don't square with the figures coming from the parent company. There's a wire crossed somewhere. I've been working on it for weeks, but I can't find anything. It looks like....."

He breaks off and shuts his mouth when three nurses enter his room. "It's time to take you in for the procedure, Mr. Newman," one of them tells him.

"Yeah, okay. I'm ready," he tells her.

I back away when they unlock the wheels on his bed and start rolling him out of the room.

He turns to face me as he passes me. "Just check it! Make sure I'm not imagining anything."

The bed turns a corner and he vanishes down the hall. He leaves me standing there with those words ringing in my ear.

The sales numbers from Cast Iron Securities don't square with the figures coming from the parent company. What does it mean?

It could mean a lot of things. It could mean an accounting error. It could mean David just isn't calculating the numbers correctly.

It could also mean some of the money Cast Iron Securities earns every month is somehow magically disappearing between here and the parent company's bank account.

We have to find out either way and I'm the only person besides David who knows about this. He can't check it. He could be in the hospital for a long time.

Actually, he already did check it. He found the error. He just didn't find the cause.

I get into my car and drive straight back to the office. The front door is still unlocked even though it's one o'clock in the morning.

I go into David's office, sit down at his desk, open all the files he has up on his computer, and start going through them one after the other looking for the smallest detail out of place.

Chapter 13: Vivian

I sit up on the edge of my bed and stare at my phone. Derek didn't call me last night the way he said he would. He said he wanted to go out for a drink and then he didn't call.

I should just blow this off. We had sex once. That's all. It obviously doesn't mean anything to him, so I won't let it mean anything to me.

I throw my phone on the nightstand, but I can't help but feel a stab of longing in my heart. I wanted something to happen between me and Derek. I saw something in him—something that could have been special.

I must have been wrong about him. I must have seen something that wasn't there—or maybe I'm just a stopping-over point for him on his way back to the top where he thinks he belongs.

I don't need that, but I still can't help getting emotional about it.

I force myself to take a shower and get ready for work. I still have to see him when I go to the office, but I make up my mind not to let it bother me. I'll just keep soldiering on and getting the job done. I don't care about him.

I won't let him use me like that again. I'll never go out with him again and I definitely won't have sex with him again. I don't need someone messing with my mind like that.

I drive to the office and brace myself when I see Derek's car in the parking lot. He always comes in early. That doesn't mean anything. He's a workaholic. That much is obvious.

David's car is in the parking lot, too, so at least I won't be alone with Derek.

I get out, go inside, and head for my desk. I don't see Derek anywhere.

I put my purse away, hang up my coat, and turn on my computer before I pick up my tablet and head for David's office to check in with him for the day.

I stop dead in my tracks when I see Derek sitting in David's chair. Derek stares at David's computer with bloodshot eyes. His eyes dart back and forth, up and down, while he clicks the mouse in rapid succession.

"What are you doing in here?!" I demand. "What are you doing on David's computer?!"

Derek looks up at me and all the color drains from his cheeks. "Oh, my God! I forgot to call you! I am so sorry, baby! Oh, I feel terrible! I should have called you from the hospital to tell you! I am so sorry! I don't know how I can ever make it up to you! Oh, this is awful!"

"What are you talking about?!" I gasp. "What hospital?"

"I was just finishing work last night and David had a heart attack. I took him to the hospital—or the ambulance did after I finished giving him CPR....."

"CPR?!!" I practically shriek. "You gave David CPR?!"

"I had to. He didn't have a pulse. Don't worry. He's alive in the cardiac ward."

"You mean......" I glance around. "So why are you here?"

Right at that moment, Sherman Wilfrey and Alistair Fiero walk into the office. Two other executives come with them. They look back and forth between me and Derek.

"What's the meaning of this?" Sherman demands. "Where's David?"

"He's in the hospital," Derek replies. "He had a heart attack last night. He almost didn't make it, but he's going to survive."

The executives spin around. "He what?" Alistair half-whispers.

"He had a heart attack," Derek replies.

"I heard you, but....." Alistair stammers. "He called us last night—at eight o'clock in the evening. He said he had to see us down here on some urgent piece of business. He said he had to see us first thing this morning with no delays."

Derek nods. "I'm not surprised. He found a trail of embezzlement between Cast Iron Securities and the parent company. He spent five months tracking it down. It's no wonder the stress wrecked his health."

"Embezzlement?!" they all gasp. "That's impossible! We check the books ourselves!"

"You apparently don't check them carefully enough. He asked me to look into it and I found all the evidence you need to tell who the embezzler is."

"Who is it? Sherman asks.

"It's you, Mr. Wilfrey."

"That's a bald-faced lie!" Sherman fires back. "How dare you?!"

Derek stands up behind the desk and turns the computer screen around so all the executives can see it.

They all stare in stark horror at the page displayed on the screen.

"This is a list of bank transactions between Cast Iron Securities and the parent company bank account," Derek tells them. "Cast Iron Securities transfers all the profits from our sales to the parent company."

He points out different transactions and scrolls down the page to display them all. "The transaction record shows all the transfers from Cast Iron Securities. They leave Cast Iron Securities' bank account just fine, but some of those transfers wind up in an offshore account with your name on it, Mr. Wilfrey."

The other executives turn on Sherman. "This is an outrage!" Alistair blusters.

"This is all a huge misunderstanding!" Sherman insists. "I can explain everything."

"You better start talking," Derek tells him. "The Police are already on the way."

Sherman spins around to stare at him.

"And I already transferred all this evidence to the SEC," Derek adds.

Sherman is still standing there gulping like a fish when a bunch of Police squad cars pull into the parking lot outside. They don't come with their sirens wailing. They pull in silently.

Officers flood the office, cuff Sherman, and lead him away. All the salespeople stand and stare in shock until the squad cars leave.

Alistair approaches the desk and holds out his hand to Derek. "Thank you. We wouldn't have found this without you."

"David would have found it eventually," Derek replies. "He was the one who originally tracked it down. He would have found it and exposed the guy."

"It's a terrible thing about his heart," Alistair remarks.

"I'm sure he'll recover. He was awake and talking to me the last time I saw him there."

"I better go check on him." Alistair pats Derek on the shoulder. "Keep up the good work. I'll come back to check on all of you later."

The remaining executives follow him out of the room. That leaves me and Derek alone together.

He eases over to me. "I am so sorry about last night. Things got away from me. I took David to the hospital and he told me about the figures not matching up. I came back here to check. I completely forgot to call you. I'm so sorry."

"It's....it's all right....I guess....."

He slips his hand into mine. "Let me at least try to make it up to you. Let me take you out to dinner tonight—not just drinks. I want to spend time with you. I don't just want to meet somewhere and be done with it."

"Um.....I guess we could."

He doesn't smile. He stares deep into my eyes. "Are you sure? I don't expect you to just forget that I totally let you down."

"It's all right." I pull myself together. "I guess it's understandable considering everything else that was going on."

"Can I pick you up at seven again?"

"Uh....okay. I'll see you then."

I stumble back to my desk too dazed to think straight. I can't even think about Derek not calling me.

So much happened last night. The office is a completely different place this morning than it was just last night.

I rest my head in my hands trying to put all the pieces together. David.....had a heart attack.....

I can't believe Derek has been right in the middle of all of this, but I shouldn't be surprised. He always seems like he's in the middle of everything.

He stops by my desk half an hour later and tells me he needs to go home and catch up on sleep. He's usually gone on trips into town during the day anyway, so the workday passes uneventfully after that—all except that David isn't here.

The office sounds spookily quiet without him here. Will he come back to work after this? Will he even survive?

I can't leave the office to find out, and by the time I finish work, I don't want to.

I go home and relax for a few hours before I start getting ready to go out with Derek.

Chapter 14: Derek

I take Vivian to a much nicer restaurant this time. I didn't tell her where we were going, but she somehow sensed it through the psychic airwaves between us.

She wears a sleek, satin black dress that leaves nothing to the imagination. The scoop neck hides her cleavage, but the dress shows plenty of her chest and graceful back swooping down to her wide hips.

She looks like she just stepped off a runway and she fits right in with the high-class clientele in this place.

I take her hand as soon as we sit down. "Thanks for giving me a second chance," I tell her.

She waves that away. "I'll let it slide this once. Just don't let it happen again."

"I don't think I'll ever have another boss drop from a heart attack right in front of me," I tell her. "At least, I better not."

"I'm really glad you were there to save him. He's a good man."

"He's great. He was more concerned about the embezzlement than he was about himself." I squeeze her hand. "I don't want to spend tonight talking about him."

"What do you want to talk about?"

"I want to talk about us—about what we're doing and where we're going."

Her whole face closes up in front of me. Her expression goes stony cold. "What are we doing and where are we going? The last time I checked, we were going out to dinner."

"This is the second time we've gone out to dinner and I spent the night at your place the other night. I want to know if it means something or if it means nothing."

"Okay," she replies with the same detached coldness. "What does it mean?"

"What does it mean to you?"

She waves that away. "I can only tell you that it won't mean anything more to me than it means to you. If it doesn't mean anything to you, then it doesn't mean anything to me. I'm not going to start caring about something that means nothing to you."

I have to take a firm grip on myself so I keep my patience. I can't expect her to soften with so many obstacles in our path.

"I'm in exactly the same situation," I tell her. "If this is all a casual good time to you, then I want to know upfront so I don't start getting invested in it."

"Would you get invested in it if I said it was more than a casual good time?"

"Of course," I exclaim. "I would get extremely invested. I might already be invested even if you do think it's a casual good time."

She lowers her eyes. I really can't stand it when she looks at anything other than me.

I squeeze her hand and lower my voice. I want to whisper straight into her brain. "Look at me and talk to me. Is this what you want? Do you want this to go somewhere—because if you do, I'm in. Just tell me what you want it to be."

She meets my eye for a split second and casts one more wild look around the restaurant. No one notices us holding hands. We look like any other normal couple.

God, I really wish we were! I want all of that with her. I just don't know if it's even possible.

"What's going on?" I ask again. "What's wrong? Why won't you talk to me?"

"You're....you have this whole business thing going," she blurts out. "You plan on going straight back to New York and getting back into The Billionaires' Club."

"So? What's wrong with that?"

"You don't even plan on staying here!" She chokes on the words. "You'll leave and I'll stay here and that will be the end of it. What's the point in us even talking about that if we can never be together?"

I stumble over the answer. "You could come with me....."

She shakes her head. "I can't. I have to take care of my mother. That's what I've been trying to tell you all along. I can't do any of that as long as she's still around."

"Well.....we could take her with us....."

She scoffs in my face. "Please. Why are we even having this conversation?"

She seals the deal by taking her hand out of mine. She can communicate so much just by that one simple, powerful gesture.

I'm still sitting there in the awkward silence trying to decide what to say to her next when the waiter comes to take our orders. We spend a few minutes talking to him before he leaves.

"Let's just not talk about it," she finally tells me. "It won't come to anything, so just leave it alone."

"So.....what are we even doing here?" I ask.

"We're going out to dinner together. That's all we're doing."

I shut my mouth and don't say anything else. We're having dinner together and that's all. We won't be going home to her place after this for another night of wild sex. We'll part ways.

We'll probably never even go out to dinner again after this. What's the point? I don't want to take her out to dinner just as a prelude to sex.

I don't want this to be a meaningless fling. I don't want to do it at all if it's going to be meaningless.

We spend most of dinner talking about work and office interpersonal dynamics. She asks me for more details about David's heart attack and how it all went down.

I take her out to my car afterward, drive her home, and walk her to the door.

"I guess I'll see you at work," I tell her.

"Yeah," she breathes. "Thank you again. I had a nice time tonight."

"I'm glad we got everything out in the open—again," I tell her. "I appreciate that we can be honest with each other."

"I really wish you all the best," she replies. "I really hope you get back everything you lost."

I shrug. "That part is easy. This is much more challenging."

She smiles up at me. It's a genuine smile of true compassion and positive vibes. "Do you want to come inside?" she asks.

I freeze when I realize what she just said. I expected her to say good night and for us to walk off in opposite directions.

Did she just ask me if I want to come inside?

"I understand if you don't want to. I just thought....." She trails off.

"You thought what? You made it clear at dinner that we were just having dinner and that's all—nothing more."

She frowns and then her eyebrows shoot up. "No, no, no, no, no! I meant the whole thing! Dinner....and whatever....."

Now I'm really confused. "You want to……"

"Only if you want to. If you don't want to……"

"I do," I blurt out.

Her eyes pop. "You do?"

"Of course. I always want to do it with you."

"Even if it doesn't mean anything?" she asks. "Maybe we shouldn't—I mean, if it's going to mean something to you and not to me."

"But you said it does mean something to you—and it does mean something to me. It might not mean we're going to be together forever, but it isn't meaningless. It means I think you're dynamite and you think I'm okay, too."

She laughs. "You're more than okay."

"I am? How?"

She won't stop blushing. "Stop arguing and come inside."

She walks away to the door, unlocks it, and I follow her inside. She shuts and locks the door behind me, puts her keys and purse on the side table, and kicks off her heels by the door before she turns around to face me.

I don't know how to approach her. I don't know how to do anything with her if it's only going to be casual.

I realize in that moment that it can never be casual between us. It never has been and it never will be. Doing it with her will always mean something. It will always mean everything.

I don't know what the future holds, but I can't let her pass me by. I can't just walk away and forget about her. That window has already closed.

Her eyes soften when she sees me coming toward her. I stop in front of her and look as deeply into her eyes as I want to. I swim in the vast seas of her beauty while I decide what to do with her—now that I'm here in her apartment.

I can think of a lot of filthy, rotten, sordid things I want to do with her, but I can't do them now—not when she looks up at me with such heartfelt longing.

This will never be casual for her, either. I see that in her eyes. She feels the same way about me. Whatever happens to us, it can never be meaningless sex or meaningless anything else.

It's important. It's crucially important.

I raise my hand. I want more than anything to kiss her, but this moment seems to mean even more than that.

I wind up trailing my fingertips across her bare collarbones to her shoulder. I let my fingers catch the thin strap of her dress and drag off her shoulder. Her dress slips a little lower on her cleavage.

Her lips fall open in a gasp of pure sensual desire. Her body and eyes burst with so much buried hunger.

I want to satisfy that hunger as never before. I want to fill her with my seed all night and see her writhing and screaming in ecstasy on my bed—except that it won't be my bed.

In that moment, I have a vision of the future. She and I live in a huge penthouse apartment with an enormous bed. We don't need soundproof walls because the penthouse covers the whole top floor of the building.

She can scream all she wants there. I can make her scream all night long and leave her whimpering and exhausted in the morning when I put on my suit and go out to conquer the world.

Then I'll come home at night and do it all over again. She can sleep during the day when I'm at the office telling everyone else what to do.

Right now, we're in her junky apartment in New Jersey and that's okay. I can bide my time until I make that vision a reality.

I glide off her other strap and her dress falls down to her hips. She's wearing a strapless push-up bra that makes her big globe breasts stand up and her cleavage nice and deep.

I sink onto one knee and slide her dress the rest of the way to her feet so she can step out of it.

She's still wearing her black lace panties and her heels. She looks like a supermodel like this—choice, juicy, and ripe for the picking.

I take her hand, lead her to the couch, and I sit down still holding her hand. I can't decide what to do first, so I pull her toward me, slide her panties down, and bury my mouth between her legs.

She moans and rocks against my face. Her fingers comb into my hair and she pulls me in tighter. I eat her faster as I feel her quickening in my hands. It's happening.

I love hearing her moan like this. I love the way she quakes and sobs as she escalates to an explosion.

I clamp my hand around her ass, pry her thighs just a little farther apart, and plunge two fingers into her.

She careens over the edge and barely stops herself from screaming as she bucks down hard on my hand. She tightens her fist in my hair and bucks her hips into my face as the waves of climax melt her body in my hands.

I stay where I am and keep licking and munching her to the ends of the earth until she wilts and staggers back. I let my fingers trail out of her, but I'm only getting started.

I pull her down on my lap and steer her to straddle me. I'm still fully dressed, but she feels how hard I am.

She grasps me between my legs and rubs me to oblivion through my pants.

I glare at her through fevered eyes. Her face shimmers with sultry lust. Her gaze keeps blurring with all the sex-drunk passion pulsating through her glorious body.

She rises on her knees, leans forward to kiss me, and starts unbuckling my belt. She unzips me, dives her hand into my shorts, and her bare hand closes around my shaft.

She leans back to look into my eyes while she strokes me. Her eyes overflow with volcanic need. She wants me. She wants me to take her and use her and make her mine.

I raise my hands, but I can't even bring myself to touch this exquisite creature. She looks like some kind of enchantress or fairy spirit sent to tempt me with all the pleasures of the flesh.

Maybe she's a demon and she's about to devour me. I really don't care.

She pushes herself up on her knees, pulls her panties aside, and sinks onto me with all her succulent juices flowing around me.

We have all night and I plan to make the most of it.

Chapter 15: Vivian

Derek curls into me from behind. He blasts heat into my back and hips when he wraps his arms around me and pulls me against him.

His hot, wet mouth falls on my shoulder in a toe-curling bite of pure, passionate hunger. I'm still half-asleep, but I already feel him getting hard.

I moan as he rocks his hips against my ass. I'm exhausted from another night of non-stop sex, but I can't help responding to him.

He tightens his grip, rolls me onto my stomach, and works his thighs and hips between my legs. I lie spread-eagled on the bed with him on top of me.

He scoops one hand under my chin and pries my head back as he spirals into me extra slow, extra hard, and extra deep.

I gasp and then start to whine and moan as he picks up speed.

His husky, tortured voice drifts into my brain through my ear. "We have to go to work soon."

I spike to the stratosphere as he plows in and twists his hips at the deepest point of his stroke. I squeal out on the brink of a massive release.

I shudder as he draws all the way out for another brutal thrust. That moment gives me just enough time to catch my breath. "I won't be able to get up with you on top of me."

He answers by driving in extra hard, but he still doesn't finish me off. He excites every inch of me, locks into my depths, and drills in even deeper there before he draws all the way out.

His slow, deliberate pace winds me up more slowly, but he winds me up to an even more powerful cataclysm once he really does release me.

"Would you like me to make you late for work?" he half-whispers. "Would you like it if I made you so late you didn't get to take a shower? You would walk in smelling like sex with my jiz dripping into your panties. Would you like to go to work like that and look across the room to see the man who did that to you?"

I gasp again as he plunges in. I can't hold out much longer.

He doesn't give me a chance to answer before he arches back and pounds in extra hard. He doesn't stop. He keeps hammering me and drives me over the edge.

He keeps holding my head up like that so he can hear me husking and choking with broken ecstasy while he wrings every last drop of pleasure from my body.

My body gives it up easily. Everything he does turns me on.

He roars in my ear building up to his own explosion, but I'm already too far gone in a sea of bliss. I keep spiraling out of my mind even after he ruptures inside me and lies there pulsating and throbbing in the throes of release.

His hot breath electrifies my mind. His hands take hold of me and move me where he wants me—right up until the moment when he rolls off me and collapses on the bed.

I curl up against his side and put my arms around him. I don't know what this means—not even after our conversation. I don't know if it means anything, but I know I want him.

I want him in my bed the next morning after we just did it all night long. I want him to talk to me the way only he can.

I don't want to let go of the only person who ever encouraged me to be something more—even though I already know I will have to let go of him.

All of this feels so much sweeter because it's temporary.

He puts his arm around me, strokes my hair, and kisses me on the forehead while we relax in bed. The minutes tick by bringing us closer to the moment when we have no choice but to get up.

He presses his lips against my hair. "Should we take a shower together?"

"We would probably never get out of it if we did that."

He laughs. "You're right. I only asked because I had designs on your body."

"Do you want to go first or should I?"

"You go first. I don't want to get up yet."

"I don't, either," I tell him. "You go first. You're the man in the house."

"What does that have to do with anything? If I'm the man in the house, I should lie here like a king while you make me breakfast and serve me in bed."

I snort with laughter and sit up. I make sure to do it on the other side of the bed where he won't be able to pull me back into his arms.

"Good luck with that." I stand up and start gathering my things to go take a shower.

"Aren't you the gourmet cooking maven?" he teases. "Who would you cook for if not me?"

I scoff in his face. "What do you think this is—a hotel? You don't get to order room service."

He smirks at me. "It's room service where the room attendants perform extra special duties for the guests."

He sits up suddenly and makes a dive to grab me. I dodge out of the way and run laughing to the bathroom.

I hear him laughing through the door after I shut it. The shower drowns out his voice.

He's already standing up and checking his phone by the time I get out. He grins at me on his way into the bathroom.

I get dressed and do my hair before I go out to the kitchen. I stop in my tracks when I see that he's already started making breakfast for both of us.

A plate with two fried eggs, toast with butter and jam, and a cup of coffee sits there waiting for me.

I wolf down the food, chug my coffee, and then whip up some bacon and biscuits while he's in the shower.

He kisses me when he comes out with his hair wet. He looks so different with his shirt off. He looks like the billionaire business tycoon I've been going out on dates with.

The disheveled, tired, hangdog salesman I first met is long gone.

He leaves first to go home so we don't show up at the office at the same time. I drive to work and open the building. David isn't here, but Alistair is.

I find him in David's office going over the documents on David's computer. "What's going on?" I ask. "Did you find something else wrong?"

He throws up his hands, straightens up, and walks out from behind David's desk. "I don't know if anything is wrong or not. Running this business isn't my thing. I need someone more knowledgeable."

"Did you ask David? I'm sure he would be happy to explain anything to you that you wanted explained."

"Where's the man who was in here before?" Alistair asks.

I frown at him. "Who? You and all the executives were in here before."

"No, I mean the other guy—the guy who found out about Sherman's embezzlement."

"You mean....you mean Derek?"

"Yeah! Him!" Alistair points at me. "I need him. He understands more about this than anyone."

"He should be coming into work any second now."

Alistair turns away and goes back to David's chair. "Send him in here as soon as he shows up. I need to talk to him pronto."

Alistair doesn't sit down. He bends over the desk and clicks on the mouse. I don't even want to know what he's looking at over there.

I go back to my own desk and start the day's work. I'm already sitting down doing payroll for the month when Derek rolls in.

He gives me the most casual, "Good morning," in history before he goes to his cubicle. I intercept him there.

"Alistair Fiero is in David's office," I tell him. "He wants to see you as soon as possible."

Derek looks up at me. "What does he want?"

"He says he can't figure out something on David's computer. Alistair says you know more about it than he does and he wants you to explain it to him."

Derek nods, puts down whatever he's working on, and goes into David's office. I go with him just because no one ever notices if I do or I don't.

"You asked to see me?" Derek begins.

Alistair waves at the screen. "You understand a lot about this business, don't you? You must if you found that accounting error and tracked it down the way you did."

Derek shrugs. "I already told you it was David who found the error. I only traced the source. That's all. He's the expert here, not me."

"David won't be returning to work. He called the executive board this morning. He's taking early retirement. The stress is killing him and he wants to spend more time with his family."

The temperature in the room drops. "I'm sorry to hear that," Derek murmurs. "Although I suppose it's good for him."

"He says the heart attack was a wake-up call and it's making him focus on what's really important. He says he spent too much time at work which took time away from his family. He won't be coming back—which means we need to find someone to replace him. You're the most qualified person in this office....."

"Now, you just hold your horses right there, Mister!" Derek fires back. "I can't take over for David! Are you insane? I'm nobody! I just rolled in off the street."

"You found the evidence of Sherman's embezzlement. I'm sure David asked you because he knew you were the one person who could follow it up and finish what he started. Come on, man. We need you too bad! Do you honestly know of another salesman better qualified than you?"

"Not a salesman," Derek replies. "Why don't you hire Vivian? She knows David's business backward and forward."

Alistair's eyes shoot to me. I can see his reaction written all over his face.

"Me?!" I gasp. "I can't take over as head of the company! Are you out of your mind?"

"Why not?" Derek asks. "You know more about this company than I do."

"Yeah, but....." I stammer.

Alistair says the words we're all thinking—or I am, at least. "I don't think the rest of the executive board would feel comfortable hiring a file clerk to replace the company CEO. If you won't do it, we'll either have to promote someone else from the sales team or advertise externally. We really don't want to do either of those things."

Derek sighs and runs his hand across his eyes. "All right. I'll do it if you insist."

Alistair hustles around the desk, grabs his hand, and shakes it hard. "That's excellent! You can start right away! Vivian, you'll reassign Derek a monthly salary commensurate with David's. You'll need to draw up a contract for his employment, now that he isn't a salesman anymore."

"Of course," I reply. "I understand. I'll take care of it."

Alistair beams at Derek and claps him on both shoulders. "This is perfect! This company is going to thrive under you. I know it is!"

He strides out of the room still glowing with delight. A pall sinks over the room as soon as he leaves.

Derek and I are finished. He's my boss now.

He turns around and his features pinch when he looks at me. "I'm sorry," he croaks.

I take a deep breath and try to shrug it off. "It's okay. The company needs you and we always knew it was going to be temporary, right?" I do my best to smile at him, but my heart isn't in it. "Congratulations. You deserved this. Alistair is right. You really are the best man for the job."

I give him one more fake smile and go back to my desk.

I spend the rest of the day drowning my sorrows in work. One brief instant in time—one conversation—and our relationship is over.

Derek is still here. He hasn't made good on his new business and he hasn't gone back to New York.

He didn't have to do any of that because our relationship was doomed from the start. It never could have gone anywhere and it didn't.

Now nothing will ever happen between us again. I'm his employee He's totally out of reach.

Chapter 16: Derek

I click a few items on my computer screen, but my gaze migrates toward the window. I stare out at cars passing on the street and my mind automatically switches back to Vivian.

I hardly remember the sex. I remember her sitting across from me at the restaurant. I remember the way she looked when we ate breakfast in her kitchen.

I remember walking next to her on our way to the car repair shop. I remember driving her home after she got a flat tire.

I could have had something real with her. I *did* have something real with her.

Now it's gone. She's gone even though she's right outside this room. She sits at her desk on the other side of that wall, but she might as well be in another solar system.

I'll never be able to fantasize about bending her over the desk or taking her in the bathroom. I'm her boss now.

Even thinking about her that way would be massively inappropriate, but I can't stop myself from thinking about it.

I don't think about any of that. I think about everything else—all the things we could have had if we built a real relationship.

Now I'm sitting here with a hole blasted through the middle of my soul. She's gone. The part of me that connected with her is gone.

Actually it isn't. The part of me that connected with her is still alive and well. That's the part of me that bleeds because she isn't here—even when she is.

I don't even know what I want with her when I say I could have had something real with her.

What we had was the most real thing I've ever felt and now it's gone. I can't even show how empty I feel without that.

Having her in the next room only makes it worse—and don't even get me started on how things go when she comes into my office to deal with company business.

This is my office now. I'm taking David's place as the head of Cast Iron Securities. I don't go out on sales calls anymore, which is another heavy blow. I was really starting to enjoy that.

I have to summon all my effort to drag my attention back to my computer. I flip through this month's payroll that Vivian just sent me.

My name is at the top where David's used to be. I'm making four times what I made before and living at the same level of expenses.

I have a lot more money to channel back into my Whirlwind launch. That speeds up the process. The business is picking up momentum and starting to take off.

The next document on my screen is the new employment contract between me and the parent company that owns Cast Iron Securities.

I start to go over it when I get a notification on my phone. It's a text from Judah Hayes.

I just saw the expose in Business Weekly *about your new venture. What do you say to coming up to New York and meeting with me and a few of the fellas who might be interested in investing in your company? Jackson and Dante say they already asked you, but maybe you feel differently about it, now that your circumstances are changing. Let me know what you think. We would all love to see you come back stronger than ever.*

I put the phone down and turn to stare out the window. Did I really think I would fly solo forever?

He's right. I did think that at the beginning, but I don't need to think that way now. My circumstances and the company circumstances are changing.

Getting outside investment isn't the same as taking the business public on the open market. I know these guys.

I also know there's no chance I would ever trade a controlling share of my company in exchange for investment. I would keep control for myself.

I absolutely trust people like Judah, Dante, and Jackson not to cut me off at the knees or throw me under the bus. I would never let Lane Prince invest in my company again, but I have no reason to think ill of any of the other billionaires from the club.

I would still make certain not to trade so much of the company that they could take me over by combining all their shares. That's the mistake I made last time. I won't make it again.

I text him back and say I would love to meet with him and the others. We set a time for this weekend.

I put the phone down for the second time. Now I really can't concentrate on work. My pulse starts racing. I'm going back to New York to negotiate a business deal with The Billionaire's Club.

It's all happening the way I planned. I didn't plan to court investors this soon, Whirlwind will build exponentially if this works. It will grow much faster than I expected.

I could wind up back in The Billionaires' Club before I know it. I wouldn't have to slave for years just to get the company off the ground.

There's still something missing, and right at that moment, as if my thoughts make it happen, Vivian enters my office.

I know what I have to do the minute I see her hips and thighs moving under her tight pencil skirt.

"Here are the sales figures from last month's closures," she tells me. "It looks like Ellie is making a move to overtake Rowan for the top spot."

"Go out to dinner with me tonight," I blurt out.

Her head shoots up. "What?"

"Go out to dinner with me tonight—unless you have something better to do."

She stares at me in shock. "I can't go out to dinner with you. You're my boss now."

"Then go out and have a drink with me as a coworker—not as anything else."

She sneers at me. "Who do you think you're fooling? You know it wouldn't be that."

I can't help but laugh. "Okay, but we can at least call it that. We can call it a business dinner where we discuss your job performance."

She bursts out laughing. "How about we discuss *your* job performance instead?

"We can discuss anything you want. Just go out with me."

She blushes so beautifully. "That probably isn't a good idea."

"Who cares if it's a good idea? Come on."

She turns bright red and walks away. "Fine. Be that way. I'll see you after work."

I can concentrate just fine after that—all except for one thing. I make reservations at the restaurant I want to take her to and then make a few other phone calls.

I leave the office first, tell her I'll pick her up at seven, and go home to change. I pick her up and we head to the restaurant.

"So how is your job performance going?" I ask once we settle in at the table.

She laughs and blushes again. "You tell me. How is the job going for you? I haven't heard any blood-curdling screams coming from the office."

"It's pretty straightforward—nothing I didn't already understand. I want you to move in with me."

Her head snaps around. "What?"

"I want you to move in with me. I want us to get serious about each other."

"We can't!" she insists again. "We aren't even supposed to be seeing each other."

"I checked the company policies on relationships. There's nothing in the fine print that says we can't be involved. You should know this."

"Yeah, but.....it's inappropriate."

"Not at all. What about these companies where a husband and wife have been married for twenty years and they run the company together? Are you saying that's inappropriate?"

"Of course not, but that isn't us. We aren't a couple and we haven't been together that long."

"But we could be. Nothing is stopping us except both of us agreeing to get serious about each other."

"We aren't going to be together that long," she counters. "You're going back to New York as soon as you can."

"This is more important. If things worked out, you could either move there with me or I could stay here and run the company from New Jersey."

Her jaw hits the tabletop. "Are you serious?!"

"That's what I'm saying. I want us to be serious about each other. I want us to start moving in that direction. I don't want to fool around anymore. All that casual stuff is just stupid. Move in with me."

Our waiter comes right then and gives her an excuse not to answer. I wait, and after he leaves, I change the subject.

I'm certain of this, now that I actually came out and said it. I want this to be serious between us.

I don't care if it takes a while for her to get comfortable with it. I don't care if it takes years for her to get comfortable with it. I'll wait.

I go back to talking about work. Then I ask how her mother is doing. I take the opportunity to ask a few more pointed questions about Vivian's family—like why she has three siblings who aren't helping out at least financially to take care of their elderly mother.

One thing I can say with one-hundred-percent certainty. I would never let my younger sister drop out of college to go work full time to support my mother. I couldn't live with myself.

I would have to step in and do something about it. I would do almost anything to keep her in college.

Vivian has three older brothers who all live out of state. They don't send money. They don't call. They don't visit, not even during the holidays.

That is absolutely criminal, but I don't tell Vivian that. No wonder she feels like she can't think about anything outside of this.

Finding out just how bad her situation is just makes me want to help and support her. I want to make this easier for her, but I also don't want to insult her by suggesting she can't do it on her own—which she obviously can.

The truth sinks in the longer I listen to her talk. I could help her by getting her to move in with me. She wouldn't have to pay her own rent. She would still have to pay her mother's rent and bills, but that would be a big load off her shoulders.

I can make this all about our relationship. She doesn't need to know this is why I'm doing it—because it is about your relationship. I'm doing it because of the way I feel about her.

We finally leave the restaurant. I sit her in the passenger seat of my car and turn the engine to switch on the heater, but I don't leave right away.

I turn to her in the parking lot. "Just think about what I said about moving in with me, okay? Take all the time you need to come to a decision. Just think about it."

"I already am thinking about it."

I lean and give her a quick peck on the lips. "That's good. I'll just wait to hear from you when you make a decision."

I shift the car into gear and drive across town, but I don't go back to her apartment. I pull into a different apartment complex.

This one has a locked, coded, wrought-iron gate blocking the driveway. I hold a code card to the electronic reader out front.

She stares up through the bars at the huge, stately, luxurious building. "Um....what are we doing here?"

"Come inside. I want to show you something."

I park and offer her my hand to help her out. I keep holding her hand when I use the same card to let us into the building.

A sliding glass door whispers out of the way leading into a tall, expensive, tiled lobby full of leather couches, fireplaces, granite coffee tables, and potted palm trees. A curved, polished wooden banister sweeps up to the second-floor landing.

I lead Vivian to the elevator. Her hand trembles in mine when we step inside and ride up to the fifth floor.

I escort her down the hall and use the same card to show her into a beautiful, modern apartment with a balcony overlooking a courtyard with a pool.

I switch on the lights and she stops in her tracks to stare at all the expensive furnishings. "What is this place?" she asks in a tiny voice.

"This is my new apartment. I can afford it, now that I'm running Cast Iron Securities and Whirlwind is taking off. I figured it was time to upgrade from that rat hole I've been living in these past few months."

I ease over in front of her, squeeze her hand, and gaze into her eyes. I wish I could somehow transmit into her how I feel about her.

"This is where we would live if you moved in with me. You wouldn't have to pay rent for your apartment anymore—but you don't have to decide right now."

She barely looks at me. She can't stop staring at everything.

I tug her hand, lead her into the living room, and pull her down next to me on the couch. "Don't think too much about it. It's just an apartment like any other. I'm still the same person and you're still the same person. Who we are and our relationship wouldn't change if we live here."

"But....but this is way too nice!" she exclaims. "I couldn't live here!"

"Why not? It means you would only have to pay rent on one apartment instead of two. I want to help you out—I mean in addition to keeping you with me all the time."

She gulps. "I don't know about this."

"What don't you know about it?" I shake that off. "Never mind. You don't have to decide anything tonight. You don't have to decide anything at all. Here. Look. I have an idea."

I open the drawer of an end table next to the couch, take out a remote, and switch on the sound system. I turn on some relaxing background piano music.

Then I stand up and go into the kitchen. I hunt around until I find some cheese and crackers, a few pieces of fruit, and a bottle of wine.

I just might have laid up this stuff in the kitchen after I left the office. I wanted to be ready when I brought Vivian back here.

It works. The music and the sound of me moving around in the kitchen breaks the tension. Vivian comes over and leans against the kitchen counter.

"When did you start living here?" she asks. "I didn't know you moved."

I smirk at her over my shoulder. "I just rented it this afternoon. I wanted to take you somewhere other than your place. I wanted to take you to my place and I couldn't take you to that other apartment. So, technically, if you really want to know when I started living here, the answer is tonight. Tonight will be the first night I stay here—so I think it's kind of appropriate that we stay here together. Then it can be both of ours instead of just mine."

I hand her a glass of wine and a plate of snacks. She takes a cracker with cheese and a sip of wine. Now we're getting somewhere.

I take everything back to the coffee table, sit down on the couch, and put my arm around her. She folds her legs under her and leans against me while she sips her wine.

This feels easy. This feels right. Sitting here relaxing with her feels better than sex.

I don't plan to keep her awake all night tonight. I just want to curl up in bed with her and sleep. I want to hurry up and start our life together—the life we're going to have from now on.

Chapter 17: Derek

I park my ratty old Camry ten blocks away from where I plan to meet the other billionaires—or just the billionaires. I'm not a billionaire anymore. I have to keep reminding myself of that.

I don't want them to see me roll up in this crappy car and I don't want to take money away from Whirlwind to buy or even rent a new one.

I'll get a new car soon. I don't need to jump the gun on that.

I check my appearance in the car window to make sure I look the part. I have to show up looking like a billionaire even if I'm not one—not yet.

I look a lot better now than the last time Jackson Metcalfe and Dante Helme saw me in public. Hopefully this creates the impression I'm aiming for.

I walk into the atrium of the Citicorp building and ride the elevator up twenty floors to the conference room. I find Jackson, Dante, Judah, and Niko Holloway already waiting for me.

I go from man to man shaking their hands. It feels good to finally come back here.

"It's so great to get you back, man," Niko tells me.

"It's great to be back. Congratulations on your wedding."

He grins at me. "Thanks. It's been great."

"We're having another club meeting on Monday," Jackson tells me. "You should come as a guest and talk to some of the other guys. We aren't the only ones who want to invest in your new venture."

I have to fight my voice under control. "Please tell me Lane isn't one of the people who wants to invest."

Dante laughs. "I think he knows better than to even suggest that."

"He does wish you well, though," Judah adds. "Seriously. You can't let bygones between you and Lane stop you from making this business a success. Don't stay away from the club just because of him—not when so many of these guys want to invest in you."

I hesitate. "I'll try to make it, but I can't promise anything. I have some prior commitments. I'll try to shuffle them around, but if I can't, I'll just have to catch up with the guys another time."

"Of course. Whatever works for you." Dante waves toward the table. "Sit down. Let's talk."

We all sit down. No one sits in any particular order or space. Everyone distributes themselves randomly around the table in no order and with no formality.

Judah leans back and swivels his chair around at his leisure. "So tell us what's going on with the venture now. Give us an idea about what you're working on and what investment would do for you at this point that you can't get anywhere else."

"I already have all the instruments and products I need," I reply. "I'm not planning to add any new ones. At this point, if anyone invested with me, I would use the money to buy advertising space and grease the wheels with a few press and industry outlets just to spread the word that these products are available. That's the thing. They're the only financial products of their kind on the market. Most of my target customers don't even know these products exist—or that they could exist."

"The *Business Weekly* spot was good for that," Jackson tells me. "You could definitely do better, though. This sounds like a job for Giovanni. It's right up his alley."

I make a face. "I would really rather not work with that guy. He's a scumbag."

The others laugh. "I won't argue with you on that, but he's a decent businessman," Dante tells me.

"He also has the contacts and the market reach you want," Niko adds. "You might not agree with his personal choices, but he's your man if you really want to reach your customers."

I roll my eyes to Heaven. "If I really have to."

"You don't have to," Jackson replies. "You can go home to New Jersey if you really want to—but from what I saw in the *Business Weekly* spot, you're just a few investors away from exploding. Don't hold back because you won't work with the right person at the right time."

"I'll make you an offer you can't refuse," Judah interjects. "If you let me invest in you, I'll deal with Giovanni for you. You never have to talk to the guy."

"I'll have to talk to him at the club, won't I?" I hold up my hand. "No, you're right. I'll deal with him. This is too important not to."

"Good for you," Dante tells me. "What else can we do for you?"

I find myself looking around at all of them. "I really appreciate you doing all of this. I really needed this."

"This is all you, man," Judah replies. "You're the one who built this company and made it what it is. We wouldn't be able to do anything if you hadn't already done the hard work."

"I want to know how we can invest," Jackson cuts in. "Enough with the pleasantries. What do we have to do to invest in you?"

"Don't you want to see the financials on the company first?" I ask.

"Of course, but I'm certain they'll all be in order. The question is how we can get this up and rolling. You've been on the shelf too long as it is."

I pull out my phone. "I'll send you the financials now. You can take a look and we'll talk about where to go next."

I open my email app and find half a dozen work-related emails. Four of them are from Alistair Fiero. It's a Saturday. He shouldn't be contacting me about business today.

I ignore them and send the Whirlwind prospectus to the four men in front of me. They all take out their phones and start reading.

I step out of the room and video call Vivian. She smiles at me through the screen. "How's New York treating you?" she asks.

"The guys are treating me great. They want me to go to a meeting at The Billionaires' Club on Monday—which means I'll need to skip work."

"That shouldn't be a problem. You should definitely stay for that."

"Alistair is emailing me. Do you know what that's about?"

She frowns. "I have no idea—but he doesn't even know I exist. Why don't you check the email and find out?"

"Okay. I just need you to tell the staff that I won't be into the office on Monday."

"Just remember we have our monthly sales training on Tuesday, so you'll need to do any preparation for that while you're up there this weekend."

"Right. I'm on it. I'll handle it. I better go."

I blow her a kiss, hang up, and go back into the conference room to find all four guys stuck to their phones.

I sit down and open Alistair's email while I wait. The executive board is having their monthly meeting on Monday. They want me to attend.

The meeting is at their headquarters office in Trenton. I can't go to that and The Billionaires' Club meeting at the same time—or even on the same day.

I email Alistair back and tell him I would love to attend, but I have a prior commitment. I apologize profusely and suggest that I attend digitally.

I hope that doesn't offend anyone on the executive board, but my Whirlwind startup comes first. These guys are right. I can't let something like this slow Whirlwind down.

The business is in a delicate place right now. I would even be willing to step down from my job at Cast Iron Securities if it meant doing what's best for Whirlwind. I can always get another job somewhere else if I have to.

"I'm going to send this through to my advisory team," Judah tells me. "They'll get back to me by the end of the day."

Dante puts his phone down. "I think we need to talk about you establishing a premises for yourself here in New York and bringing in new employees—admin staff, sales staff, call center people—all of that. If you're going to advertise and spread the word over the widest possible bandwidth, you'll need the infrastructure to service those customers when they come a-knocking."

"That was going to be my second point," I reply. "So far, I've been courting customers one at a time—but I need to streamline my training process. I don't want to just bring salespeople on board and let them do whatever they want."

"You need Kevin for that," Jackson tells me. "He can handle anything when it comes to personnel."

"I don't want to use Kevin to hire staff," I correct. "I want to do that in-house so we have more control of who we get and what qualities fit with the company mission. These products are going to take a certain kind of salesperson to promote them correctly. I don't care how much experience someone has. Any salespeople who come on board need to go through training so they understand the products and how to promote them the right way."

Dante nods. "Absolutely. I completely agree with you."

"That will take time," Judah remarks. "What you could do is take the investment capital you get from us, start your onboarding process, and get your salespeople fully trained and ready before you run the ads."

I blink at him. "You want to invest? Are you sure? You said you were going check with your advisory team."

"I have to get their signature on it, but I'm sure they'll agree with me that this is a promising investment opportunity—and you're behind it." He smiles at me. "I have the utmost confidence in you—and this prospectus is perfect. I don't see anything wrong with it."

"I'm in, too," Niko tells me. "I've been looking for something like this."

I look from one man to another. "Thanks. You don't know what this means to me."

Judah stands up. "Let's go get some lunch. We can talk more casually there—as friends, not investors."

We walk out of the conference room and talk about Whirlwind on our way to the elevator—or I talk about it while they listen.

I can talk about Whirlwind all day and all night. The guys don't interrupt. They let me go on at length.

I don't want to monopolize the conversation, but they keep prompting me with questions so I wind up launching into another long speech about whatever they just asked me.

We wind up at a hole-in-the-wall Chinese restaurant where everyone is Chinese. The five of us are the only non-Chinese people in the place—and the waiters barely speak English.

All four of my lunch companions start brainstorming about how I'm going to start training my salespeople and bring in new customers at the same time.

I have to race to keep up with all the ideas flying around and interject with information and considerations the guys have to consider so they come up with the right combination of strategies.

I feel like I'm at the UN or something. These guys couldn't be more helpful and supportive. Just sitting here with them and talking everything over—it's good for my soul.

This is going to work. I'm going to get back on top. It's nice to know I'll be in good company when I get there.

Chapter 18: Vivian

I set up the computer in the conference room. Rowan, Isaac, Ellie, and all the other salespeople are already in there waiting.

Derek isn't here. I haven't seen or heard from him since Saturday. I don't know if he even remembers that we have a meeting this morning.

It's already ten o'clock in the morning—or it's five minutes until ten o'clock in the morning. The meeting starts at ten.

He should have come back to town by last night at the latest, but he hasn't called me or even texted me.

Don't ask me what I'll tell the salespeople if he doesn't show up. Maybe I won't have to say anything. None of them knows what's going on between me and Derek—if anything is going on between me and Derek.

The salespeople won't think to ask me why Derek missed the meeting. They'll probably just speculate—like they do with everything else about him.

They still don't know who he is. The pool keeps rising on what he did before he started working at Cast Iron Securities.

Ten o'clock strikes. The salespeople sit down. Then they all look around at each other. Derek isn't here.

He bursts in at the last second all breathless and windblown. He's wearing his fancy suit—the one he wore to New York—the one he's been wearing on all our dates. He looks like a million bucks—or a billion bucks, more like.

He pants out apologies and says he just got back to town this minute. He hustles to the front of the room, turns on the computer, and launches into his presentation.

He's teaching the salespeople about body language. He seems extremely prepared. He pulls up a detailed PowerPoint slideshow to illustrate all the details he wants to educate them on.

If I didn't know any better, I would guess he spent the whole weekend working on this—but I already know he didn't.

He speaks smoothly, calmly, and effortlessly once he catches his breath. He puts the room at ease and even makes the salespeople laugh at certain points.

I watch him from the back of the room. None of the salespeople comment on how well put together he looks compared to the way he's been dragging himself in here every day since he started.

He looks like the boss. He looks like he knows enough and is confident enough to take charge of this company, but he does it subtly and casually so he doesn't ruffle any feathers.

He concludes the meeting with question-and-answer time. I take the opportunity to slip out of the room and return to my desk.

I stay out of Derek's way for the rest of the day. I don't know what's going on with him, but whatever happened to him in New York doesn't include me.

He gets into a phone call with the executive board later in the afternoon. He's still on the phone when I leave for the day.

I'm on my way out to the car when he runs out to catch up with me. "Vivian!" he exclaims and pulls up in front of me. "Thank you for covering the office yesterday. I really appreciate it."

"No problem," I tell him. "I was just doing my job."

"Did you think about what I said about you moving into my apartment?"

"I don't think that's a good idea. In fact, I don't think it's a good idea for us to see each other anymore at all."

His face goes white. "Why? What happened?"

"You're obviously being pulled in too many different directions. I don't want to live with the uncertainty of thinking you might leave or that something might happen that's more important to you than the relationship."

"Nothing like that would happen because nothing is more important than the relationship."

"You say that, but your actions say the opposite."

"I don't understand. What did I do? I told you I was going to New York and I told you I was going to stay there over Monday. I told you I was going to be here for the sales meeting and I was."

"What have you been doing ever since your meeting ended on Saturday?" I ask. "You've been off the reservation for three whole days without one word to me about where you were or what you were doing."

"The meeting on Saturday never ended. That's why didn't call you. I've been in non-stop meetings with members of The Billionaires' Club. They all want to invest in Whirlwind and we had to talk about all of it and what I'm going to do with their money and how it's all going to work out. We kept talking until late on Saturday and then again on Sunday. It was too late to call. Then I went to the club on Monday and I had a video conference with the executive board before I drove back here."

"You could have texted me. You could have texted me even if it was three o'clock in the morning to tell me what was going on and that you at least didn't want me to worry about you."

He gulps. "I'm sorry. I didn't even think of that."

"That's exactly what I'm saying. You go on about married couples that have been together twenty years who run companies together. Do you honestly think any of them would go out of town for three whole days without at least texting their significant other to tell them what's going on so they don't worry."

"I'm sorry," he chokes. "There was just so much going on....."

I turn back to my car. "There was just so much going on that was so much more important to you than I am. You made time to have a video conference with the executive board, but you couldn't make the time to send me a single text in three whole days. Don't worry. I understand. You have your priorities in order. Just keep doing what you're doing. You'll get back into the club and everything will be rosy for you."

I open my door to get in and drive away. I really need to put as much distance between me and him as possible.

"Don't walk away from me, Vivian," he insists. "I'm serious—and I want us to be serious."

"You want to be serious, but you aren't serious. You aren't stable enough for a relationship. I don't know if you ever will be, but you definitely aren't now. I'll see you later."

I get behind the wheel, slam the door, start the motor, and drive away.

I drive to my apartment building, but I don't go inside yet. I stay there in the parking lot, cover my face, and take some deep, shuddering breaths.

That was the hardest conversation I've ever had, but I have to stand firm. I can't let him treat me like a hobby or a side project he'll come back to when he feels like it. We're either together for real or we aren't.

If he does something like this now, he'll do it during a relationship. If it wouldn't be okay for him to ignore me then, it isn't okay for him to do it now.

Thank the stars I didn't get serious about him or move in with him. Thank God I didn't become dependent on him to lighten my financial situation. I couldn't deal with that.

Chapter 19: Derek

I gaze through the limo windows at the flashing lights of Broadway gliding past the car. People in fancy clothes walk back and forth in front of the theaters out there.

Damn, it sure feels good to be back and enjoying the finer things in life. I'm on my way to attend a Billionaires' Club gala. I'm going as a guest, but at least I'm going.

I'll get back into the club in no time—especially with the way Whirlwind is taking off. The other billionaires are giving me all the support and help I could ask for—and it's working.

I get heart palpitations about going to the gala. These events used to feel so ordinary back in my heyday. I never got excited about them.

I always felt like I was just going to hang out with my friends. We would talk about our businesses, shoot the breeze, and eat and drink the same way we did at the club.

We just did it while we were wearing tuxes. That was the only difference.

This is the first time I've worn a tux since I left New York. I don't feel like an imposter. I already know I belong here.

I just feel like I'm stepping back into a life I used to find so familiar.

It will feel familiar again—some time. It will just take me some time to put this suit back on and get used to it.

The limo turns onto 45th Street and then onto Park Avenue before it stops in front of the Empress Hotel. The gala is taking place in the grand ballroom.

I go in and check with the doorman. He already has my name on the guest list.

Kevin Drake meets me right outside the ballroom entrance doors. He bursts into a huge smile and shakes my hand. "Hey! The prodigal returns."

I snort. "Hardly. I'm only here as a guest."

"Let's not fool ourselves about that. You're going through our trial period."

I look up. "I am?"

"Of course! Didn't you know?"

"No. I just thought......"

He waves that away. "We're all following your meteoric rise back to stardom. You'll get back into the club. These are just the preliminary formalities. We'll let you back in with no extra hoops to jump through as soon as your net worth hits a billion."

I gulp and look away. "I didn't know. I don't want you to give me any special treatment."

"No one is giving you any special treatment, my friend." He claps me on the shoulder. "Come on inside. You've been gone for too long."

He leads me into the ballroom. It's already packed with men in tuxes and women in formal evening gowns draping to the floor.

All the women glisten with diamond jewelry. They look incredible—but no one of them can hold a candle to Vivian.

I become painfully aware that I'm here by myself. I can't count the number of galas I've attended by myself.

Half the guys in the club are unmarried. They bring different dates with them at different times. Sometimes the single guys even hire escorts to bring with them so the guys don't show up alone.

I didn't do any of that—and I don't want to. I don't want to be here with anyone but Vivian.

Kevin takes me over to a group where Giovanni Nowaczyk is talking to Niko Holloway, Rory Khan, and Zane Vancroft.

I'm already in negotiations with Giovanni to promote Whirlwind as soon as my new sales staff is ready to handle the incoming workload.

The guys are all talking about a completely different project Giovanni is working on. I'm just catching up on the conversation when Melody Gottlieb comes over to us.

She slips into the circle and slides her thin, shapely arm around Niko's back. He puts his arm around her shoulders and kisses her on the temple while the other guys talk.

She smiles at me across the circle. "Hello, Derek," she murmurs. "I didn't know you were going to be here tonight."

I find myself smiling back at her. "It's great to see you, Melody. I'm sorry to hear about your father. I hear you're a member of the club now."

She turns bright red and her eyes dart around the group. "Don't tell anybody."

The others laugh, and right then, Zane's wife Dana glides over to join us. She's a member of the club, too.

The conversation shifts. The guys start talking about some deals they're doing together. Then Dana and Melody get involved.

They start talking like they're part of these deals and have decision-making power over what happens, when it happens, and how it happens.

I don't know why I'm surprised. I already knew Niko and Melody got married, that her father died and she inherited his fortune, and that Zane and Dana were a rising power couple in the club.

My gaze migrates the rest of the way around the ballroom. The place pulsates with energy, especially from the women.

They're beyond beautiful, but that isn't what bothers me. I know some of them.

Actually, I know quite a few of them. Melody and Dana aren't the only female members of The Billionaires' Club to come to this gala.

Some are single and bring their male dates. Others are married, either to other billionaire members of the club or to men who aren't members of the club.

Me being here on my own means something completely different now. The club hasn't changed since I left. It's the same club it was before. I just see it differently. I see my place in it differently.

I would have thought nothing in the past of bringing any random girl to a club gala. I never hired an escort because I didn't have to. I just brought whatever girl happened to throw herself at me that week.

I can't do that anymore. I need a woman on my arm, but not just any woman will do—not anymore.

I need a woman I can grow with. I need a woman who does for me what Melody obviously does for Niko and Dana obviously does for Zane.

It seems so obvious, now that I really look with new eyes. I see Judah and his wife, Piper. They stand with their arms around each other while they talk to the guests.

Judah and Piper look so different. He looks so much darker standing next to a woman with such pale, ivory skin. She's so much shorter than he is. She makes him look enormous—even bigger than he usually looks.

He makes her look tiny, but I have never seen Judah so happy. He radiates a kind of inner peace I've never seen in him before.

She glows with pleasure, too. Her eyes sparkle and her cheeks flush. Everyone knows Piper Lagrange. She's one of the most highly respected lawyers in Manhattan, but she's all woman standing next to her husband.

My world comes to a grinding halt when I see Lane Prince standing across the ballroom with Samantha Mulholland.

She isn't Samantha Mulholland anymore. She married him. Everyone knows that.

They aren't standing with their arms around each other. They don't need to. They occupy a corner on the opposite side of the room from me.

They lean together and murmur in each other's ears about people in the room, who's talking to whom, and who belongs to which companies and business associations.

He says something that makes her laugh. Their eyes meet—and that's the moment when I fully realize the depth of their love for each other.

I didn't see it before—probably because I didn't stick around long enough to find out.

I was too absorbed in how much Lane did me wrong—and how Samantha betrayed me by cooperating with the hostile takeover—as if she could do anything else.

I always admired and respected Samantha. What's not to admire and respect? She's brilliant, honest, kind-hearted, and she stayed committed to the company.

I see the takeover differently now, too. I shouldn't have suggested that she turn her back on the company.

I wanted her to quit her job in solidarity with me, but I only thought that because I was a selfish prick who insisted on feeling sorry for himself at the expense of the people he was supposed to care about.

I never would have suggested that or even thought it if I really cared about her. She put her lifeblood into that company. She did what was best for the company, not what was best for me.

I don't blame her for that now. I applaud her for it. It only proves what an exceptional person she is.

She got the happiness she deserves with Lane. He's the better man because he could give her that.

I never thought of her that way and now I don't resent either of them—for any of it. I can't even resent him anymore. He did what he did and it's in the past.

I probably could have stopped the takeover in the first place if I hadn't been so stubborn about negotiating with him. I had a thing about him, so I refused even to consider selling the company.

None of that matters anymore because I'm on my way back. I will become a member of the club again. Kevin is right about that. I know it. He knows it. Everyone knows it.

There's just one thing missing. I need Vivian. I don't want to come back to the club or New York without her.

I wave to the people around me, say a quick, "Will you please excuse me for a minute?" and head for the entrance doors.

I get my coat from the coat check guy, ride down the elevator to the street, and take a cab across town to the 24-hour parking lot where I left my car. I get in, turn the motor, and take off driving on my way back to New Jersey.

Chapter 20: Vivian

I lift my head, shut my eyes, and let the sun shine through my eyelids. It's still cold, but at least the sun is shining.

Children's laughter makes me look up at the kids playing and screaming on the jungle gym in the park. My mother walks around the edge of the lawn poking in the flowerbeds and looking at all the plants.

The flowerbeds don't have any flowers in them or even really any plants. It's still the middle of winter, but she smiles to herself, pushes a stick into the leaves, and stirs them around before she goes off exploring somewhere else.

I wait for her to finish. She doesn't get out of her apartment much. She needs fresh air and time outside. I can wait before I drive her home.

Someone sits down next to me on the bench. I move down a few inches to give the person more room.

Without warning, the person says, "Maybe she should get a job here so she could garden the way she did at home."

My head whips around and I wind up staring at Derek sitting next to me. He's wearing business casual clothes—not his fancy suit or the untailored one he wore when he first moved here.

"What are you doing here?" I snap. "I told you I didn't think it was a good idea for us to see each other anymore."

"I just happened to be driving past. Actually, I was on my way to your apartment when I saw you, so I decided to come over and talk to you here."

"What do you want?" I don't even try to keep the resentment out of my voice. "Go back to New York where you belong."

His eyes go soft when he turns to gaze across the park. "I did go back there. I went back there this weekend for a Billionaires' Club gala. They all insist that I'll become a member again and I'll get back to where I was before."

I try not to grimace even though he isn't looking at me. "Good for you," I grumbled. "I'm sure you'll be very happy there with all your money and your rich friends."

"I won't be happy there with my money and my rich friends because I'm not going back."

I spin around fast. "What?"

"I'm not going back. I don't want to go back without you. I don't want to live without you. I would rather stay here and keep working for Cast Iron Securities—forever if I have to. I don't care what I do as long as you're with me."

He turns around and locks his eyes on me. I've never seen his eyes so soft and overflowing with emotion. He doesn't try to hide that from me, either.

He barely speaks above a whisper. "I decided last night that I'll shut down Whirlwind if you really want me to. I don't care what it takes. You're more important than all of that."

"But.....but that's your dream! You couldn't turn your back on that!"

"If you're okay with it, I'll keep doing it from here. If you aren't, I'll shut it down. I might start doing something else, but I won't do anything that interferes with us."

He slips his hand across the bench and clasps mine. His hands are always so warm.

"You said you wanted to know what was going to happen with us. You said we couldn't get serious because I was going to leave New Jersey and you didn't want to." He shrugs. "So that's what we'll do. If you don't want to move to New York, we'll stay here. That's all. I want to commit to you. I want my commitment to you to come before everything else. Whirlwind means nothing to me without you. I wanted it because I wanted to prove I could get back what I lost. I proved to myself that I can and I did. I don't need to go all the way. I can let it go, but only if I get you in exchange. It will be worth it if I do t hat."

"But...." I can't stop blinking at him. "You're serious."

I don't even know why I say that. I've never seen him so serious.

Every word out of his mouth strikes a hammer blow on my heart. He would turn his back on all of that for me.

He must be really serious. He's talking about making a much more life-changing commitment than just moving in together.

I can't look at him. I have to turn away and stare out at the park while I take it all in.

His soft voice drifts into my brain. "If you tell me you aren't interested, I'll walk away right now and you'll never see me again. I'll quit Cast Iron Securities so you don't have to deal with me again. I'll recommend to the executive board to bring you on to run the company. You'll make more money than you know what to do with. You won't have to worry about paying your expenses and your mother's expenses. Heck, you might even move into that apartment I rented."

I cringe at those words. He would really do all of that for me. He would take care of me and my mother even while walking out of my life forever at the same time.

I'll never find another man who cares about me this much. I'll never find another man who would go to such lengths for me and sacrifice so much for me.

I can't let him go. I need him too much—and not because he's taking the burden off my finances.

He would let me keep doing that if I really wanted to. He isn't trying to make me dependent on him.

That's the thing that really stings. He encouraged me to start my own business doing something I'm passionate about.

I can't remember anyone else ever suggesting that. Not even my high school guidance counselor suggested something like that.

Derek is the only person who cares. He would encourage me to do that even if it meant I made more money than he does. He doesn't care how much money either of us makes. He just wants me to be happy.

He pulls his hand out of mine. "Okay," he murmurs. "I tried. I'll go call Alistair right now and tell him......"

"NO!!" I whip around. "Don't! Don't leave! I.....I don't know what to say....I don't even know how to answer you.....but don't leave. I.....I don't know how to do any of this....."

He sinks back on the bench and his features melt when he finally looks at me. "You don't have to know how to do any of this. Just tell me you want to do this with me."

"I don't know....I don't even know what this is.....what you're asking me to do....."

"Say you'll give me a chance if I stay here. Say you'll be willing to go ahead with our relationship if I'm not being pulled away in multiple directions like you said. I'm here. I'm going to stay here. If you want to, we can keep working together for a few months just so you can see that I'm really going to do this......"

"A few months?!" I practically shriek. "You would keep working together for a few months so I could see if you're really doing this?!"

"Well, you tell me. What do you need to see or hear or find out to prove to you that I'm sincere? Do you want me to shut down Whirlwind......?"

"No, Derek!! How can you even ask me that?!"

"Well, how am I supposed to know if I don't ask you? So you would be okay with me running the company from New Jersey? Would you be willing to get back together with me as long as I told you I planned to stay in town for the rest of eternity?"

I gape at him with my mouth open. I can't even form words.

This is beyond anything I ever expected from him. He has been bubbling over with excitement and new energy over the prospect of going back to New York on his victory lap of Billionaire Central.

Now he's talking about throwing it all away. He talks about it like it's no big deal. He makes it sound like he would be willing to do so much more—so much I would never in a million years ask him to do.

"Will you please talk to me?" he murmurs. "I can't read your mind. Tell me what is going on with you. Tell me what you need me to do so we can move forward."

I collapse back on the bench and cover my forehead with my hand. "I can't think. You tell me what you want to do."

"Okay, if you really want to know, in the ideal scenario, you would move into the apartment with me. Either you can continue to support your mother out of your wages from the office or I can take them over for you—depending on which you feel most comfortable with."

I clamp my eyes shut. He is not talking about taking care of my mother.

"If you really don't want me to shut down Whirlwind, I'll keep doing it from here. I'll stop going up to New York—or at least not so often. I'll move our operations down here and I'll conduct negotiations and stuff remotely."

"I don't want you to shut it down," I croak. "You should pursue your dream even if you do it from here."

He slips his hand across the bench and covers mine again. He lowers his voice even further to a confidential half-whisper.

"In the end, I would like to see us get married and live happily ever after. I would like to see us buy a piece of property where you can grow your garden and cook all your favorite foods and live the life of your dreams. I can't think of any better use for this money. To me, that's the only reason to do any of this."

Tears sting my eyes at those words. He would really do all of that—for me. He has no experience with any of that. He wants to give it to me to make me happy.

I have to keep this man. That's all there is to it. I just have to make this work somehow.

"What do you want me to do—today, I mean?" I ask.

"That depends on whether you're okay with all of this."

"Of course I'm okay with it." My voice cracks. "How could I not be? You're offering me everything I've ever wanted."

"Then the question is if you want it with me or with someone else."

"Of course I want it with you," I counter. "I always wanted it with you, but you never offered that before. You never offered any of it."

He shrugs. "You're right. I never realized until last night that I wanted it. Now I know. I don't want to wait any longer unless you want me to so you can feel comfortable with it. I don't want you to do anything against your principles or anything like that....."

"Will you stop saying that?! I want to, Derek."

He frowns. "You do?"

I groan and cover my eyes. "Yes, Derek. I do."

"Then....what do *you* want to do today." He hesitates. "Do you want to come home with me—to the apartment?"

I look away and go back to watching my mother. "I guess so. I have to drive my mother home and then I should stop by my place to pick up some of my stuff."

He doesn't answer. He has to work hard to suppress a look of wild excitement flashing through his eyes.

He satisfies himself with just say, "Okay. We'll do whatever you need to do and go at your pace."

He doesn't say anything else and I don't break the silence. I feel him busting with energy. This was more than he dared to hope.

He really would have walked away if I told him to. He would have quit his job and left town to make sure I felt comfortable living here without him.

I don't know how to deal with a man who cares about me this much. I've never dealt with a man so committed before.

No one has ever even suggested sacrificing for me—not even a little bit. I'm not sure I'm comfortable with him sacrificing this much.

Chapter 21: Vivian

Derek and I sit in silence holding hands for half an hour before my mother stops where she is and looks around at the playground and the park. She no longer smiles at the frozen flowerbeds.

Now she looks anxious and uncertain. I mumble under my breath, "I gotta go," pull my hand out of his, and walk over to her. "Come on, Mom. It's time to go home. Are you cold? We can make you some hot cocoa when we get back to your place."

The uncertainty drains from her features when she sees me. I lead her toward the parking lot.

We have to pass the bench where Derek sits by himself. He watches me lead my mother away. Then he follows us to the parking lot.

He stands next to his old Camry and watches me open the passenger door, put my mother in the seat, and help her buckle the seatbelt.

He waits until I get behind the wheel before he does the same thing.

He follows me across town and parks near me while I go inside and settle my mother into her apartment. We share a cup of hot cocoa before I wish her good night and leave.

He's still sitting in his car waiting when I get outside. He follows me back across town to my place—my old place.

He comes inside with me this time. "Do you need me to help you pack anything?" he asks.

"No, I'll only take a few things now. I'll come back after work later to get the rest."

"What about your furniture and everything?"

"None of this is mine. The place came furnished. I don't have that much stuff. It will fit in the new apartment just fine."

That's the whole conversation. He sits on the couch until I come out of my bedroom with my clothes and toiletries packed into my duffel bag.

He follows me back outside and we drive to the new apartment—our new apartment. I set my duffel bag on the floor by the front door and ease into the living room while I take it all in.

This is going to take some getting used to. I might never get used to it.

I'm used to working all the time to pay for everything. I have a hard time wrapping my head around the fact that I won't have to pay rent next month.

I'll have to give notice at my old apartment. Then I won't have to pay for it anymore. I don't know how to think about or even accept that.

I stand by the balcony doors and look down at the courtyard and the pool surrounded by lounge chairs, umbrellas, and trees.

The pool and the lounge chairs are all covered for the winter. The umbrellas are all tied and folded up to protect them from the weather.

No one is down there swimming right now, but they will be. I could be one of them. I could go down there and swim on hot summer days. I could sunbathe. That would be something.

It would be something I've never done before. I never gave myself permission to relax and enjoy my life that much.

"What do you want to do about dinner?" Derek asks me from the kitchen. "We could go out again—or we could stay in. What do you feel like? I could cook for you—but I might need to make a run to the grocery store first."

"I don't want you to cook," I reply without turning around. "And I don't want to go out, either."

"You don't? What do you want to do?"

I turn around extra slowly to face him across the room. "I want to do the cooking. I want to cook for you."

His eyes fall out of their sockets. "You do?"

"Of course I do, Derek," I murmur. "I told you I like cooking. I told you I'm passionate about it. I just never had anyone to do it for."

He won't stop gaping at me. "I didn't mean you would do it for me. I mean.....I'm only one person."

I laugh at him. "You're my person. Who would I do it for if not you?"

He gulps. "Only if you want to."

"I do want to. I've been waiting for a chance like this." I walk over to the kitchen and push him out of the way. "Stand aside."

He laughs, but only nervously. "Should I be worried about this?"

"Only if you don't like eating." I pull open the fridge. "Now let me see here......"

Now he really does laugh. He turns to walk away. "I don't want to be around for this."

He goes out to the living room and messes around while I search the fridge, the pantry, and the cupboards.

This place is stocked with all the usual cutlery, utensils, plates, glasses, and flatware. He has a good supply of groceries, but I see a few things missing.

I get a piece of paper and pen out of my purse and start making a list. I'm starting to get excited about finally having someone to cook for. This is going to be fun.

Derek brings his laptop, phone, tablet, and a yellow notepad over to the kitchen counter. He sets up to work there while I go through all the kitchen cabinets one after another.

"What do you think you'll make?" he asks.

"What kind of food do you like?"

He pauses and then says, "Yes."

I laugh. "Very funny."

"You said it. I do like to eat, so whatever you put in front of me, I'm sure it will find a home."

I cock my head to study him while I think it over.

"What?" he asks.

I shake it off and go back to what I'm doing. "Nothing. I was just thinking."

"Obviously. Just tell me you weren't coming up with a new recipe for napalm."

"I could probably make some serious money on that." I pull a bag of rice out of the pantry. "Let me guess. You never really got into cooking, did you?"

"Is it that obvious? Maybe you could give me some tips."

I find myself staring at him as a million ideas come together in my mind.

The first words that come to my mind to answer him are, *You'll have to watch my YouTube channel.*

Did I really just think that?

If I'm really going to do this—if I'm really going to commit to him and cook for him and make a life with him—if I'm going to whip up some mind-blowing tasty dishes to win my way to his heart through his stomach.....

Why not video-record myself doing it? Why not turn it into something?

He's right about one thing. I have absolutely no reason not to.

It would cost me nothing to do that. My cellphone already has a professional quality camera on it.

I might have to buy a tripod or something to set up the camera, but that shouldn't be too expensive.

I don't have to pay my mother's rent anymore. A tripod should be peanuts compared to that.

My mind goes into a tailspin thinking of all the possibilities.

He said he wants us to get married. We would probably wind up having children.

He said he wants to buy a piece of property so I can have a garden and cook our meals from that. He wants us to live the way I lived growing up.

Our children would grow up that way. That's what he says he wants.

If I did all of that......

The idea of video-recording all of that—documenting it—sharing it with the world—sharing all my tips, tricks, and life lessons—

Thinking that gives me a surge of excitement unlike anything I can possibly imagine.

Cooking for Derek is just the beginning. It inspires me to express my creativity this way, but now I see a whole world of possibilities beyond just him.

This is so big it scares me. I can't even tell him.

I can't tell him I plan to buy a tripod. It scares me too much to buy a tripod.

I can't do any of that. How could I? How could I ever get big enough for that? I'm nobody. I don't even know how to upload a video to YouTube, much less shoot it, light it, or edit the video beforehand.

I shut my eyes and shake that out of my head while I work. Derek doesn't notice.

I cringe when I see him working on his laptop. He's up to his neck in building his own dream empire.

It all seems to come so naturally to him. I know that isn't true. He started selling comic books on the street when he was just a kid.

Now he's running what could be a billion-dollar company—and it isn't the first time. He must have learned all of that somewhere.

I could never do something like that. I can't even overcome this mental block to ask him.

He would tell me. I know he would. He would be more than happy to tell me everything I want to know. He would help me. He would guide me. He would support me every step of the way.

I can't do that. I can't even bring it up.

I feel like an idiot—first of all because of everything I don't know. I have a high school diploma. That's it. That's the only thing I have going for me.

I could never be like him. I'm just not built that way.

I prefer to linger in the background. I would die if I ever saw myself on camera or put myself on the internet. God no.

I distract myself by making dinner for both of us. I make Pad Thai curry with roti on the side. I try to put the whole YouTube idea out of my head, but it keeps coming back to haunt me no matter what I do.

I keep imagining how I would do all of this if I was recording myself doing it. I keep hearing myself narrate an explanation of what I'm doing, how I do every step, and why.

This idea simply will not leave me alone. Now it's driving me crazy.

Derek gets so consumed with his own work that he doesn't notice anything I'm doing. He doesn't even notice me setting the table.

I don't want him to notice. I don't want him to treat this as anything out of the ordinary. I want him to get so used to me cooking that he doesn't even see me doing it anymore.

He would definitely notice if I set up a camera and started talking into it. I could never do something like that if he was going to be anywhere around where he could hear me. That would make me too nervous and self-conscious.

I try for the millionth time to put the idea out of my mind. I don't need to think about it because I'm not going to do it. Never in a million years.

Chapter 22: Derek

I stand up, shut my laptop, and get out the power cord to plug it into the outlet under the kitchen counter.

Vivian keeps working between the sink, the counter, and the stove. I don't even know what she's making. I don't dare to ask.

I want to show her how happy I am that she's here, but I don't want to interrupt.

She finally heads for the table to put out some hot pads on the table to hold her pots and dishes and whatever. I have to make my move now.

I walk over to her just as she's bending over the table. I wrap my arms around her from behind and nuzzle into her hair. "I'm really glad you're here. I wouldn't trade this for the world."

She hugs my arms and then breaks away just as fast, but she shoots me a smirk over her shoulder while she hustles back to the stove. "Hold that thought."

I laugh. "How long should I hold it?"

"As long as you think you can stand it. Why don't you decide what you want to drink for dinner? You looked like you had a stash when I came over last time."

She's right. I open the pantry and unlock the wine chiller. "What are we having?" I ask.

"Thai—medium heat—with that chicken breast you had in the fridge. Should we be having a white with that?"

"Sounds like it. What's the sauce base?"

"Peanut and tomato."

"Yeah, it's a white."

"I don't know about all that wine stuff. That will have to be your area of expertise."

"What—you didn't become a trained sommelier in your free time while you were pushing paperwork at the office? I'm shocked."

"My parents didn't drink. They were strictly against it, so I never learned. I only know a little bit from what I could pick up here and there."

I take the bottle and two glasses to the table just as she comes over with a huge pot of steaming, saucy goodness I don't even recognize.

"Holy Jesus!" I exclaim. "Who are you planning to feed—the Red Army?"

She laughs and blushes. "Now you know why I never cooked just for myself. I have a tendency to go overboard."

"There are only two of us. How do you expect us to eat all of that?"

She shrugs. "We can freeze it and take it for our lunches when we go to work. Home-cooked food is better for you than eating out anyway."

I shake my head as I sit down and open the bottle. "I don't foresee us eating out ever again at the rate you're going."

She laughs, brings over a dish of rice, and then a bowl lined with a cloth napkin. It's full of small, round, fragrant flatbreads.

"This is absolutely incredible," I tell her. "I feel like I'm in a restaurant."

She won't stop blushing at me when she stands next to my chair, drapes a napkin over her wrist, and bows at the waist. "May I serve the gentleman?"

"Stop fooling around and go sit down. I should be the one serving you."

She giggles and sits down opposite me. Then she looks around. "Now what do we do?"

I hold out my hand. "Give me your plate."

She hands it over and I serve her a big pile of rice with a scoop of the sauce and meat over the top. I stick two flatbreads into the side of the pile and hand it over.

"I'm going to have to start going on a diet if we eat like this," she remarks.

"I'm sure you'll always be stunning to me."

She blushes again and we start eating. I have to stop myself from falling out of my chair when I taste the food. It tastes like I'm in a restaurant, too.

I can't believe I've been seeing her all this time and never realized how talented she is.

I have to do something about this. I have to channel this passion of hers into something.

I wish I could get her interested in the idea of starting a YouTube channel, but I don't want to turn off her passion by pushing her to do something she isn't ready for.

I already dropped the idea once and she shut it down. She'll have to pick it up on her own if she does it at all.

Maybe cooking around the house will get her back into it.

I don't feel right about her doing this only for me. She should share this with the world. It's too big.

It almost feels important that she do this. She's sitting on a massive well of talent she has never expressed before.

I really hope she hasn't been holding back because she thinks she isn't good enough—or because she thinks she's a nobody or something like that.

No one has ever encouraged her before. No one ever told her she could. No one ever believed in her enough to give her a chance.

Her family seriously let her down by letting her quit college. That still rubs me raw, but I'll probably never meet any of them anyway.

She doesn't express any interest in seeing them again—for obvious reasons. I wouldn't want to see anyone like that, either.

"So?" she asks after a while. "What's the verdict?"

"I think you belong on TV," I tell her. "I think Martha Stewart should be sitting at your feet taking lessons."

She blushes and lowers her eyelashes. "It isn't that good."

"No, it's better—but you already knew that. You know you're good. You know you're great. You're beyond great. You're a superstar."

"I am not!" she exclaims. "Not even close."

"You're a superstar in seed form. You're a superstar who hasn't started to sprout yet—but you will. Then look out, world."

She giggles and puts her food in her mouth so she doesn't have to answer.

That's okay. I'll just keep dropping hints and encouraging her. I won't push it.

I'll be right behind her if she does it. I'll be right behind her if she does anything—even if she just looks up on the internet how to do it.

Baby steps. It all starts with baby steps. She'll get there, now that the door is opening for her.

She'll start to see another world of possibilities and I'll be there to watch her blossom. I can't wait.

We finish eating and she stands up to clear the table. I point at her. "You sit down. This is an equal-opportunity household. You did your part. Now it's my turn."

She narrows her eyes and hisses through her teeth. "Ooo! I love it when you get all commanding and dictatorial."

"I'm not being dictatorial. Fair is fair. You cooked. I clean."

She laughs and takes her wine glass to the living room. I start clearing the table, packing up the food to put in the freezer, and putting the dishes in the dishwasher.

"We're going to need more freezer space if you keep cooking like this," I tell her.

"Keep some of it out for lunches."

"We'll need some more appropriate containers for that, too." I pull open the cupboard and hunt around for containers I can use for what we need. "I can see this kind of life is going to require some different planning and organization."

"I started a shopping list—over there by the espresso machine. See?"

"Ah, yes. Of course. I should have known you would be all over it." I jot a few things on her list. "We can add to it as we go along."

She beams at me across the room. "This is going to be great. I'm excited about this."

I smile back at her. I don't tell her just how excited I am about this.

I'm especially excited by how excited I see her getting. She's coming to life in ways I never imagined.

I would have insisted much sooner that she move in with me if I knew it would be this good for her—but I guess I was the one who wasn't ready for it.

I pack up the food, clean the table, and scrub out all the pots and pans. Then I wipe down the counters and the stove, throw the dishtowels in the laundry, and sweep and mop the kitchen.

I get so into what I'm doing that I don't notice how quiet it's getting in the apartment. I find out when my turn comes to carry my wine glass into the living room.

I discover Vivian stretched out on the couch sound asleep. Her half-empty wine glass stands on the coffee table waiting for her to pick it up.

I sit down on the opposite couch and watch her sleep. I just want to sit here and admire her beauty—especially the beauty inside her.

She takes care of everyone else. Now it's my job to take care of her.

This is why I came back from New York—this right here.

All the money in the world can't buy this feeling. All the money in the world can't buy the conversation we just had about freezing the leftover food and buying better containers so we can start taking her leftovers to work for lunch.

Life doesn't get better than this—building something real with the person who matters the most. I hope I can be that person for her.

I want to be a lot more than that. I want to be her biggest cheerleader. I want to be the person who lifts her enough that she actually thinks her dreams are possible.

I send up a silent prayer that I can help her make that happen, but it has to come from her. I can't give her the dream. She has to be the one who does it—and she will.

I know that now. She will do it. She just needs the fertile ground of love and support to fuel her inner desire.

I have to be patient with her. The seed of her dream has been living underground for a long, hard, cold, brutal winter.

It will take time for me to give her enough warmth and sunshine before the seed starts to grow. I might not even realize right now how long it will take and how much of an investment of love and acceptance she needs.

I have all the time in the world. I have the rest of our lives to give her everything she needs, even if she just needs to sleep right now.

I leave her where she is and bring my phone and notepad over to the couch so I can work while I watch over her.

This feels so unimaginably good. I never let myself believe I would ever find something that means more to me than Whirlwind does, but she definitely does.

She doesn't wake up. She must be more exhausted than I realized. She really has been carrying the world on her shoulders. She's been carrying that responsibility almost her entire adult life.

Darkness falls outside and she still doesn't wake up. I go into the bedroom, unpack her suitcase, and put her clothes in the closet and in the dresser.

She brought a pair of pink pajamas with kittens all over them. How cute.

I lay out her pajamas on the bed, pull down the covers, change into my own pajamas, and go into the living room.

I lift her up in my arms. "It's time to go to bed, sweetheart," I murmur. "Come on. Tomorrow's another day."

She whimpers in her sleep and wraps her arms around me. I never want to lose this feeling.

I lay her in bed, take her shoes, socks, stockings, and jacket off. I unpeel every layer. I barely see her body. I just want her to be happy, healthy, and comfortable.

She wakes up just enough to change into her pajamas before she burrows deep into bed.

I turn off all the lights, crawl into bed with her, and wrap my arms around her. I don't even want to do anything with her. This is too good the way it is.

Chapter 23: Vivian

I stop in front of a store window and point through the glass. "What about those for our lunch containers?"

"They're a little too big, aren't they?" Derek asks. "No way could you eat that much in one sitting. You'll never be able to convince me of that."

I can't help but laugh. "You clearly have never seen me eat when I really want to stuff my face."

"I'm not sure I want to see that. Keep being the dainty little lady I think you are. Don't shatter my illusion—not yet."

He slips his hand into mine and laces our fingers together. We stroll on to the next store. It's a kitchen supply place with every gadget and gizmo known to man.

"Do you need anything for the kitchen?" he asks.

"Besides more containers? You have enough."

"Are you sure? I don't want you to struggle."

"I like to keep things simple. I like to make it work with the basics."

He grins at me. "I love that about you."

I smile back at him and blush. Was that his backhanded way of saying he loves me?

He didn't say it, so I pretend it wasn't. We leave the kitchen supply place and pass a department store. "What about clothes?" he asks. "Or underwear—or any of that feminine stuff I'm too ignorant to know exists?"

I laugh again. He always makes me laugh. "I wouldn't tell you if I needed anything like that. I would sneak out and buy it behind your back."

"Good idea. Leave me to rot away in my ignorance."

"Do you want to tell me anything you need of male stuff I'm too ignorant to know exists?"

"Hell no! Are you crazy?"

We both laugh at the joke and turn a corner on our way down another block. "There's a movie theater over there," he suggests. "Do you want to stop and watch something?"

I frown at the sign over the building. "They're showing the original version of *Godzilla*. I think I'll pass."

"Where should we go next to look for lunch containers?" he asks. "We've exhausted all the available possibilities."

"Not all of them. There's a storage company down on Cambridge Avenue."

"Oh, yeah. I forgot about that. Let's go They're bound to have something."

We turn around to head back toward his car. He still hasn't said or done anything to replace his Camry.

We turn back around the same corner. I go back to window shopping, but he stops dead in his tracks.

I look over at him and see him staring at two men coming toward us from the other direction. I don't know either of them.

One is a really tall, broad-shouldered black man with a shaved head. The other is much younger and shorter, but the younger one has a hawkish, almost predatory look in his eyes.

I have to slow down to match Derek's pace. He walks slower and slower as the men come closer.

They eventually stop facing each other. Derek eyes both of these men and they eye him. Derek stiffens. I can't tell if the other two do.

The black guy nods. "Derek. How you doing?"

"I'm good," Derek replies. "How are you doing?"

"I'm good, too." The black guy's eyes dart in my direction and he nods to me, too. Both of these guys can see me holding hands with Derek in an obviously intimate way.

The black guy says a very polite, "Good morning, Ma'am."

I reply by saying, "Good morning."

"Vivian Cooper, this is Judah Hayes and Niko Holloway," Derek interjects. "They're both members of The Billionaires' Club. Judah and Niko, this is Vivian."

Niko says, "Nice to meet you."

"We missed you at the club breakfast last Sunday," Judah goes on. "Jackson says he invited you."

"Yeah, he invited me," Derek replies.

"Giovanni says he was supposed to meet with you then to talk about moving forward with your marketing," Niko adds. "You skipped out on three other club events where you were supposed to discuss your upcoming moves with other club members."

"I had to leave New York for something more important," Derek replies. "I contacted all of those people to arrange to handle that business remotely. I've decided to change my plans. I won't be moving back to New York the way I planned. I'm going to run Whirlwind from New Jersey."

Judah narrows his eyes. "Do you mind explaining to us why you chose to take that step? Don't you think you at least owed us an explanation after all the support we've given you—not to mention investing in this company?"

"I'm grateful for your support and I'm sure you can all see that your investment dollars are still working toward the company the way we originally planned. The company's fundamentals haven't changed just because it will be headquartered here instead of in New York. I'm still working with all the members of the club I was working with before. Nothing about our communication has changed except for the platform we're using. I'm sure you guys communicate with people electronically every day."

"Of course we do, but we had a right to know of such a fundamental change in the company's structure," Judah insists.

"Like I just said, the change doesn't affect the company's fundamentals at all—but I'll explain it to you because I like and trust you guys and I have nothing to hide from you." He squeezes my hand. "I decided to stay so I could be with Vivian here. She supports her mother who isn't in a position to leave town. Vivian doesn't want to move away from her mother and I don't want to move away from Vivian."

Both Judah and Niko look over at me. I squirm in my skin under their intense scrutiny. Are they deciding if I'm good enough for Derek to throw away his whole business for me?

He isn't throwing away his business. These men might be billionaires and captains of industry or whatever they are, but surely even they must realize that his business is still just as good.

"Are you sure you want to do this?" Niko asks.

Derek compresses his lips in the slightest show of annoyance. "I'm quite sure both of you would gladly walk away from all your wealth and power to keep your wives. I'm sure Zane and Lane and all the others would do the same thing. I'm not going to throw away what could be my one chance at happiness for a fistful of dollars. I can run the business just as well from down here. Family comes first. Live with it. I was building Whirlwind on my own before you guys stepped in. I can do it again—but you don't need to do that because nothing fundamental has changed about the business. You know it hasn't. I'm still meeting with everyone I need to meet with and hitting all the targets and milestones I'm supposed to hit. I really don't know what more you want me to say."

Judah looks down at the pavement and changes his tone to a husky murmur. "You're right, man. I would give up anything to keep her."

"It sure would be nice to see you back at the club, though," Niko adds. "It sure was great to see you getting back on the horse. It seems a shame to waste that."

Derek shrugs. "A lot of things would be nice. I don't need to ride around the streets of Manhattan in a limo going to black-tie events. None of that is necessary for me to run my business. This is necessary. It's all about priorities."

Judah finally nods. "I understand now. I sincerely wish you the best. I'm sure we'll continue to do business, but like Niko says, it sure would be nice to see you around more often."

Derek says, "Thanks," and holds out his hand to shake with both of them.

They shake his hand back before they walk away in the direction from which they came.

Derek and I stand in silence for a minute. He doesn't break the silence while he stares after the two men.

I don't interrupt his thoughts before he rouses himself and sets off walking down the sidewalk again.

He only notices me a few minutes later, glances in my direction, and immediately looks away. "Sorry about that. I'm sure it won't happen again. They'll go back to the club and tell everyone about my decision. No one will question it again after today."

"Are you sure you really want to do this?"

"Of course!" He spins around and pulls me to a stop. "I don't ever want you to doubt me again. I don't care about any of that. We're more important. Your mother is more important and your sense of wellbeing is more important. It doesn't matter if you need to stay in New Jersey because of your family obligations or just because you feel better here. We're staying. That's all there is to it. It isn't even a question."

"Maybe you really should go. This is where your heart lies."

"My heart lies with you. I won't go back without you. I told you that. Anyway, we already had that conversation. We don't need to have it again."

He turns to walk away for the second time. Now I'm the one who pulls him to a stop. "No, I mean it. You should go—I mean *we* should go. They're right. You can't run Whirlwind from New Jersey—I mean, you could, but it would work so much better if you were there. You'll be able to meet with other club members more often. Staying here isn't what's best for the company."

"Staying here is what's best for you and for us," he insists. "That on its own makes it the right decision. The company exists to make us happier, richer, and better able to make our dreams come true. We don't exist to serve the company. It doesn't work that way."

I look deep into his eyes. "You need to go, Derek. You're passionate about this project. You can't let something like this hold it back." I squeeze his hand. "I'll go with you."

His eyes pop out of his skull. "You can't do that! You would have to quit your job!"

I shrug. "I can get another one there if I really have to......but you said....."

He raises his eyebrows. "I said what?"

I struggle against agitation and finally blurt out, "You said you would help take care of my mother. You said you would take over.....if I needed you to....."

"Of course I will! I would absolutely take over. Is that the only reason you don't want to come to New York? You said you didn't want to live that far away from her—and you don't have to. We can stay here. It's no big deal."

"It is a big deal! Whirlwind is a big deal. It's as big a deal to you as my mother is to me. I don't want you to give it up."

"I'm not giving it up. I'm still doing it. Staying here doesn't stop me from doing that at all."

I throw my head back and square my shoulders. "No. You need to go to New York. You need to be there in the middle of everything, so that's what we'll do."

He frowns. "Are you sure? I don't think I feel comfortable with this."

"I'm sure. We should go."

He won't stop furrowing his brow in concentration. "Hmmm."

I squeeze his hand. "Come on. We can still do all the things we planned to do. Nothing is stopping us. Let's go home and we can start planning everything."

Chapter 24:
Vivian

Derek and I walk into our apartment. He's carrying two big shopping bags loaded with all our new food storage containers.

He puts them on the counter and we both start peeling off the labels, removing all the other packaging, and putting the containers in the dishwasher along with their lids.

"These are going to be perfect," I exclaim.

He stops what he's doing, moves in behind me, and pushes me over on the kitchen counter from behind while he gnaws into my neck.

"You're perfect," he growls in my ear.

I feel him starting to get hard. His hands slid down between my legs from the front, but my skirt gets in the way.

He rubs against me for a minute before he breaks away and goes back to folding up the shopping bags.

I start the dishwasher with the new containers inside and put away the rest of our groceries and other items we bought in town today.

He walks around the counter and sits down on one of the barstools with his laptop in front of him.

"How do you feel now about the idea of moving to New York?" he asks while I work.

"I'm feeling more comfortable with it the more I think about it. I mean....." I look around the apartment and wave my hand. "This apartment could be anywhere. Who we are inside these walls won't change just because we moved cities, right? New Jersey isn't that far away. I can come over and visit my mother as often as I want to."

"What about working for Cast Iron Securities?" he asks. "How do you feel about quitting that job?"

"I don't feel anything about it. I don't care about the job."

He looks up. "You don't? But you've been there for years."

"I've been there for years and never gotten close to anyone there. You and David are the only people I ever even talked to and I never got close to him. Now he's gone and you and I are together. The job doesn't mean anything to me."

"Okay. I didn't know that. I thought you were really dedicated to the company."

"I was dedicated to the idea of earning a steady income and supporting myself and my mother. I dedicated myself to that and doing a good job so I could keep doing it. I made myself valuable to David and helped him as much as I could. That's all."

He stops what he's doing, rests his elbows on the counter, and studies me over his laptop. "Do you remember when I offered to recommend you to take over the company after I left?"

"Yes, I remember."

"Does that interest you? Would you get more interested and more dedicated to the company if you knew something like that was a possibility for you? Does that inspire you or get you excited or motivated to stick around?"

"Not really. I would only be interested for the extra pay. It wouldn't make me more dedicated to the company than I am right now—if that's what you meant."

He looks down at his screen. "That is what I meant. Thank you. That answers my question."

"Why do you ask? What's on your mind?"

"I just wanted to explore your thinking and make sure moving to New York really was the right decision for you. I wouldn't want to take you away from Cast Iron Securities if there was still some possibility you could find your niche there—but it sounds like that isn't the case."

"I have no reason to dedicate myself to the company—not as anything other than a place where I earn a paycheck. It isn't like securities and financial products are really a special interest or passion of mine. They might be for you, but they don't really interest me at all."

He nods. "I see that now. I understand."

I let that go, take some of our purchases to the laundry room and bathroom, and come back to the living room to finish up. I should probably start planning what I'm going to make for dinner tonight.

I happen to pass Derek from behind. He's on the internet looking at pictures of what look like houses.

"What is that?" I ask.

"I'm checking the real estate listings for apartments in New York—where we could move." He points to the screen. "Take a look. This one even has its own billiards room, pool, and home gym."

I gape at the pictures on his screen. "But....we could never live there! Those are like....they're like mansions!"

"They're penthouses." He flips to another one. "This one has an in-floor jacuzzi in the master bedroom with big windows overlooking Central Park. See? Imagine us in the jacuzzi late at night.....with all the city lights in front of us.....candles around the floor......glasses of champagne in our hands.....soft music playing....."

His eyes snap to me. The picture on the website doesn't look as romantic as he makes it sound. The picture looks luxurious, but kind of sterile.

He paints a picture in my mind of us naked in the jacuzzi sipping champagne in the candlelight.....

A charge of electric arousal grips me when I think that. He and I would definitely be the same in that apartment. Nothing would change.

We would crave each other there. We would savor every minute of our time together. We would explore all the hidden layers of our relationship and fall more deeply in love every single day.

I look up into his eyes and can't resist the allure of his unbending gaze. He reads my desire in an instant, wraps his arm around me, and pulls me between his knees.

We fall together kissing for the ages. I want him all over me and for me to be all over him. I want him to take me everywhere in that penthouse apartment and get our love for each other all over it.

I love him. I know that now and I know he loves me. He doesn't even have to say it.

He says it in a thousand ways. He says it when he encourages me to be more than just an admin clerk in someone else's business.

He says it when he explores my deepest needs and feelings to make sure I have everything that will make me happy.

He takes care of me better than I take care of myself. He watches over me and makes me feel safe and protected.

His lips explode with energy the minute I think that—or maybe I'm the one who explodes with energy.

That feeling goes off in a cascade between us. It keeps building and never stops—just like us.

He pulls me on top of him, pushes up my shirt, and steers my knees on either side of his hips to straddle him.

This position turns me on beyond anything I've ever known. I can't stop riding him even with all our clothes in the way.

This passion we feel for each other consumes all my doubts. Whatever happens to us, wherever we go or wherever we wind up—I'll keep craving him and surrendering to him no matter what. I can't get enough of him.

He pulls me in so much faster and harder than I'm ready for. He crams me down on his hard spike, drills up into my saturated panties, and then tugs them aside to fill me to overflowing

I stare into his eyes as he propels me to the stars. We could be in our new penthouse right now. We could be in the jacuzzi or on the couch or in bed or on a barstool at the kitchen counter.

The rest of the world disappears. Nothing exists but him and me and our bodies coming together in this tempest of pure desire and matched craving.

Chapter 25: Derek

I pace the floor of the new call center in the new Whirlwind Investment Assets headquarters.

It occupies four floors of an office tower in Midtown Manhattan. Whirlwind doesn't own its own building yet, but that will happen sooner rather than later considering the way things are going.

I listen to our newly trained sales staff on the phone with prospective clients and customers. Sales are pouring in from Giovanni's marketing campaigns. The company's net worth keeps rising.

I follow each salesman's pitch, presentation, and the questions they ask. All these people have gone through the training program I specifically created for this company. All these people know what to do to stay in line with our company ethos and sell our products the best way.

I climb the stairs on my way back to my new office. I have to fight myself not to constantly check the sales stats and all the company financials.

I've worked hard and gotten a lot of help to put all the pieces into place. Now I just have to sit back and watch the dominoes fall.

I'll be the first person to find out about it if something goes wrong. Then I'll be the one to step in and fix it.

I get halfway up the stairs when I get a notification on my phone. I pull it out. The notification is an email from the official Billionaires' Club email address.

I open the message.

You have been invited to a meeting of The Billionaires' Club as a guest of

Kevin Drake

Please reply to this message to confirm your visit.

It's a standard, form email the club sends out to guests who have been invited by one of the members. The message gives the time and day of the meeting. It's the day after tomorrow.

My heart starts racing. Why is Kevin inviting me to the club? He's the membership officer. Is he letting me come to one of the club meetings so he can invite me to re-apply for membership?

He shouldn't. My net worth isn't a billion yet.

It doesn't matter because I know I'm going to go to that meeting. I sit down at my desk in my office and send him an email back thanking him and accepting his invitation.

I can hardly sit still for the rest of the day. I'm busting with excitement by the time I get home to the penthouse I share with Vivian.

We got the one with the in-floor jacuzzi. We've even christened it since we moved in.

She's still unpacking all the boxes we brought from New Jersey. Neither of us had that much stuff, but the combination of hers and mine makes it seem like more.

I can't stop talking about Kevin's invitation the minute I get through the door.

"Who's Kevin?" she asks.

"He's the membership officer for the club. I'm not doing business with him, so he wouldn't have invited me unless he plans to let me re-apply. My net worth isn't at a billion yet, but maybe they want to start the process because I'm so close."

She frowns at me. "Did we meet him outside the department store that one time?"

"No, the black guy was Judah Hayes and the other one was Niko Holloway."

She shrugs her eyebrows and goes back to taking the kitchen supplies out of a box. "I can't keep track of all these people I've never met before."

"You'll meet them at the next open event. It will be great when you finally get to know everyone. They all know about you after our conversation with Judah and Niko. I want you to meet the other women, too."

Her head shoots up. "What other women?"

"The other women from the club."

She stares at me in shock. "There are women in the club?!"

"Of course. Women can become billionaires, too, you know."

"Yeah, I know, but......" She turns away. "I never thought about that before."

"Melody Gottlieb is a member now. She's Niko's wife. She inherited her father's fortune and now she's running all of his companies. Then there are the other guy's wives. Most of them are involved in the business world one way or the other. You should meet them."

She doesn't turn around. She mumbles under her breath. "I guess so."

I go back out to the living room to do some more work on my laptop. Knowing I'm that close to getting back into The Billionaires' Club gives me more motivation than ever to take this company to the top.

I can barely contain myself for the next two days before the club meeting. I'm not nervous. I'm just really happy that it's finally happening. This is the culmination of everything I've been working for since I moved to New Jersey in the first place.

If I get back into the club, I will finally understand that my success really is my own doing. It doesn't matter anymore if circumstances knock me back down into the gutter where I have to start over again from zero.

I can start over from zero. I can start over from zero anytime, anywhere, anyhow. Nothing will ever stop me again.

I take a bunch of deep steadying breaths before I walk into the club. Everyone is already there talking, hanging out, eating, watching TV, and doing everything else they always do at club meetings.

Club meetings are just social times for all the billionaires to hang out, talk business, not talk business, and just enjoy each other's company.

I spot Kevin talking to Jackson, Lane, and Giovanni on one side of the room. I go over to them and shake hands with Kevin.

"You made it!" he exclaims. "Welcome, welcome, welcome. A thousand times welcome."

"Just once is enough. Thank you for inviting me."

He claps me on the shoulder. "Let's plan on you attending next month as a member."

I catch him staring back at me just as intently as I'm staring at him. He doesn't look away.

He really means that. He wants me to reapply.

Whirlwind is pushing a billion-dollar net worth, but I'm not. I might hit a billion by the next meeting. He must be planning to fudge it to because it's me.

I can only whisper, "Thank you," but the other guys distract us.

Jackson shakes my hand and then Lane steps forward with his hand out. He smiles at me with genuine warmth. "Congratulations. It's great to see you back."

I have a hard time holding eye contact with him. "Thanks," I mumble. "Congratulations on your wedding—and everything else."

He bursts into a grin. "Thanks. I hear you might be going that way, too. I'm happy you found the right one. It's a minefield out there."

"Thanks," I murmur. "She's a keeper."

"That's wonderful. So what's her line of work? Is she in the business?"

"Not in that way. She worked for the company I worked for while I was building Whirlwind, but she gave it up when we moved back to New York. She's starting her own enterprise now."

He nods and says, "That's great. Good for her."

I don't tell him or these other guys that Vivian hasn't even started her own enterprise yet. She's dabbling if she's doing anything.

I don't even know anymore if she will start anything. Maybe she'll just be happy to explore her interests and passions on her own and never take them out on the open market.

I'm okay with that as long as she's happy. I shake hands with Giovanni next.

"How are the new call center people working out?" he asks.

"They're doing a great job. We have a forty percent conversion rate on the ads you created for us. We're hoping to increase that, but we're happy with it for now."

"You should be," Jackson tells me. "It's a great starting place."

"How are you fixed for investment capital?" Giovanni asks.

"We don't need any additional investment right now. We're converting enough sales to fund ourselves now. Some of the people advising me still want me to take the company public, but I'm resisting.

I don't see any reason to when the company is already growing this fast without it."

"I don't blame you," Jackson replies. "I would probably never feel comfortable taking a company public ever again if I went through what you went through."

"You could take the company public without losing your controlling share," Lane interjects. "You could keep fifty-one or fifty-two percent of the shares for yourself and never sell. That's how Apico got you in the first place. No one person held all the shares. We wouldn't have been able to take you over if you did."

My head shoots up. He says it so casually—like we're talking about any other aspect of our business.

He's the one who stabbed me in the gut in the first place. He's the reason I had to start over from zero and spend months living hand to mouth before I clawed my way back to the top.

Now he's giving me advice on how to stop it from happening again? Really?

He doesn't act like it's any big deal that he's helping me and advising me. He acts like he understands perfectly, too.

Is it possible I could consider him an advisor, too? Is it possible I could ever consider him in my corner as much as any of these other guys?

Judah and Rory come over just then. They distract all of us, especially when Judah, Jackson, and Giovanni start going over every detail of my business.

The three of them have been intimately involved in helping me launch the company and getting it to this point.

They get so into it that Lane and Kevin wind up wandering off to the buffet. The subject of the Titanium Finance takeover doesn't resurface.

I can't hold it against Lane—not anymore—not after today. He's willing to put it behind us and so am I.

He wants to help me learn from it. He wants to help me protect Whirlwind from going through the same thing. I can only respect him for that.

I would be stupid not to accept his help. He knows more about the acquisitions world than I could ever learn. Who better than to ask about how to prevent someone from acquiring Whirlwind?

Chapter 26: Derek

I smirk at Vivian in the back of the limo. "You look sensational."

She squirms in her sleek black ball gown. "I feel like a tart."

I burst out laughing. "Tart? Do you mean the kind you eat or the kind you hire on the street?"

"Both." She leans forward, twists her body in knots to do something to the back of her bra strap, and wriggles on the seat again. "I shouldn't have worn anything so revealing."

"You look great. You don't look trashy at all. You're going to fit right in. All the women wear dresses like this."

"I don't like this." She tries to hike up her bra and the top of her sleeveless gown a little higher. "I shouldn't have come."

"Of course you should have. How else are you going to get to know everyone?"

"I'm not sure I want to get to know everyone. I just want to stay home and live my life in peace." She gasps out loud. "This whole business is way over my head."

"What business? You aren't involved in the business."

"Not that business. I'm talking about all of *this*—the penthouse, the club, these galas. It's all too much. I'm not a part of this world and I don't want to be."

"I thought you liked the penthouse."

"It's too big. It's like a museum or a train station or something. It isn't a home."

"What do you want to do about it? Do you want to go back to New Jersey? We already opened the Whirlwind headquarters in Midtown."

She looks away and squints out the window. "I know. You definitely belong here."

"I belong wherever you are. If you really want to, we can move back to New Jersey and I can commute to town every day. Lots of people do it that way."

She makes a face, but the limo pulls up to the hotel just then. I get out first, offer her my hand, and help her out.

She looks radiant in her sleek black gown. She wears a teardrop necklace resting in her cleavage. Her hair tumbles over her shoulders in magnificent waves.

I know the truth when we walk into the ballroom. She's easily the most beautiful woman here.

She takes a step closer to me when she sees all the guys wearing tuxes, all the women wearing formal dresses, and the waiters hustling everywhere to serve food and champagne to all the attendees.

I make my way into the crowd, shake hands and greet a bunch of people, and introduce Vivian to everyone who comes over to us.

She shakes hands and tells them it's nice to meet them, but she doesn't try to talk to anyone. The guys from the club come over to talk to me about the latest Whirlwind news.

Vivian doesn't say a word. Niko arrives at the gala with Melody on his arm. She smiles and welcomes Vivian. So does Samantha.

We see Judah and Piper at a distance, but they're too busy talking to other people.

The evening wears on. I get Vivian a glass of champagne and a plate of nibbles for both of us to share. We stand in one place while all the other attendees come by to greet us and pass the time.

I'm just finishing catching up with Diego Espinosa and Dante Helme. They leave and Vivian murmurs in my ear. "I can't do this."

I turn to face her and the bottom drops out of my world when I see tears in her eyes.

"What's wrong?" I ask. "You're doing great. It's natural that you don't feel totally comfortable here when you don't know anyone, but you'll get to know them in time. Why don't you go talk to some of the women on your own."

"No...you don't understand...." She casts a frantic look of pure terror at all the gorgeous people around her. "I can't do *this!* I can't do any of this! I don't belong in this world. You do, but I don't. I can't live in a big fancy penthouse like that. I can't hang out with people like this. I can't have this be what passes for your social life."

She waves at everything again and passes her hand across her eyes.

"This whole thing—this whole relationship was a bad idea," she chokes. "I'm going back to New Jersey where I belong. I can get my job back. Just forget all about this, Derek."

I stare in abject horror as she spins away. She really is leaving.

I dive in front of her to stop her. "Don't do this, Vivian!" I have to fight my voice under control. "What we have is too good. We can move back to New Jersey together. We can go back to the other apartment. We can even move into your old apartment if we have to. You can't leave! I need you. Don't throw this whole thing away."

"No. I have to do this." She chokes on sobs. "I should have known from the beginning that it couldn't work. I did know, but I fooled myself. You belong in this world. I don't. You built your headquarters here. You can't leave now. Just forget it, Derek. Just leave me alone."

She rushes out of the ballroom and leaves me standing there in shock. How can my whole world come tumbling down around my ears right now of all times?

Whirlwind is riding high. I'm riding high. I'm getting everything I ever wanted—except her.

None of this means anything without her. I never should have agreed to move back to New York. I knew that, but I didn't listen to my instincts.

I can't lose her. I really meant it when I said I would shut down Whirlwind just to keep her.

What if I can't keep her even if I do shut down Whirlwind?

I'm not sure anymore if I *could* shut down Whirlwind. It's too big now with too many other key people involved. They wouldn't let me shut it down—and I don't want to.

I want her *and* I want my success. I don't want to give up either one.

Vivian isn't here anymore. She's gone—maybe for good. I turn away. I want to leave, but that means going home to the penthouse.

She said she wants to be alone. Is she taking some time to reconsider—or is she at home packing up her stuff to go back to New Jersey?

I should talk to her, but not to try to get her back. I just need to wish her well and make sure she has everything she needs to get her life back.

She needs her space right now. That's the least I can give her.

I stumble across the ballroom to the balcony overlooking Park Avenue. I gaze down at the lights and people below me. Why am I even here? I don't want to be here without her.

I can't remember ever feeling this bad about anything. I really just want to shut the doors on Whirlwind tomorrow morning. I hate it if it could cost me the one thing that makes my life worth living.

I just have to talk to her. I'll need my business to take my mind off my heartbreak if she really does leave.

Someone comes up behind me and touches me on the back. "Are you okay?" a soft female voice murmurs.

I look up. It's Samantha. She gazes up at me with all the warmth and softness I remember. She made working with her so effortless.

She puts me instantly at ease. I always know exactly where I stand with her. Everything must be okay if she's here next to me and looking up at me like this.

That feeling doesn't change, now that she's married to another man.

"I just saw Vivian run out," she murmurs. "Did something happen?"

I can't look at her, so I look down at the street again. "She doesn't feel like she belongs here. She feels out of her depth here—but she sees that I belong here. She wants to go home to New Jersey—without m e."

She squeezes my shoulder. "I'm so sorry. Do you want me to talk to her? Maybe it would smooth things over if I made friends with her."

My eyes shoot up. "You would do that?"

"Of course. This is her very first time meeting everyone. How is she supposed to feel comfortable here? She should meet us in a more casual setting."

"I don't know if she'll listen. She seems pretty set in her decision."

"Then you have nothing to lose, right? Just let me try it. It can't hurt."

I look back down at the street. "Thank you. I don't deserve your help after the way I acted toward you."

"Stop it," she murmurs. "You were out of your mind. You're okay now. Besides, someone has to do something about Vivian. We can't let her throw all of this away just because she doesn't feel comfortable here. She isn't the only woman who came from humble beginnings."

"Thanks," I mumble. "I'm really happy for you. Lane is a lucky man."

She beams at me and pats my arm. "I have a really good feeling about you and Vivian. You two obviously love each other a lot. The rest of this will work out one way or another. I'm certain of it. Why don't you go home and talk to her? I'll take care of everything else."

She glides back into the gala and leaves me uncertain. I don't know what she could possibly accomplish and it isn't like I can do anything about it anyway.

This is Vivian's decision. If she leaves me, she leaves me. I'll just have to deal with it.....somehow.

Chapter 27: Vivian

I flop down on the couch, cover my face with my hands, and burst into tears. I didn't let myself cry all the way home from the gala.

I can let it all out, now that I'm inside these four walls.

I don't know why I even call this penthouse home. It isn't a home. It never will be. It's a lifeless tomb or maybe a closet.

It echoes every time someone takes a step on the tile floor. It's cold and heartless. I can't live here.

I never should have agreed to move here. I always knew it wouldn't work out between me and Derek. We had too many problems from the beginning.

I really wanted it to work, though. I really loved him, but some obstacles are too big even for love to overcome.

I cry my eyes out for fifteen minutes. I could cry for a lot longer, but this dress is too damn uncomfortable.

I never should have let him convince me to crowbar myself into this outfit. Everything about it feels wrong.

I don't even give myself a chance to stop crying. I storm into the bedroom, strip off the dress and all my straitjacket lingerie underneath, and throw everything into a pile on the end of the bed. I don't even try to treat this stuff gently. I'll never wear it again.

It's too late for me to leave the penthouse tonight or even to start packing. I change into my pajamas, yank the bedspread off the bed, and drag it out to the living room to curl up on the couch. No way will I sleep in that bed tonight.

I start crying again once I cocoon myself on the couch with the bedspread wrapped around me. I'll never sleep in that bed with Derek again. That hurts.

I finish crying the second time. I can't cry over this anymore. I just have to get busy tomorrow and get my life back to the way it was before.

I can't rely on anyone else to take over my responsibilities. That was my first and last mistake—thinking someone else cared about my life as much as I do.

My life is my responsibility—no one else's. I never should have depended on Derek or anyone else for that.

It doesn't matter because I know I can do it. I can get another job if Cast Iron Securities doesn't take me back. My experience there will be more than enough to get another similar position.

I'm just thinking about curling up and going to sleep when the door opens. Derek comes in, sees me wrapped up on the couch, and sits down on the couch opposite me. He doesn't come near me.

He stares at me in silence for a long time. I don't even want to know what he's thinking.

"Are you all right?" he husks after a while. "I won't try to talk you out of your decision. Just tell me if you're all right. Do you have everything you need? I'll call Alistair in the morning about you going back to work. I have to go into the office tomorrow morning and then I'll drive you back to New Jersey. You still have your apartment. You can move back in and start paying your own rent the way you did before. Will that work for you?"

I nod down at my hands. I feel too awful to cry even when he's treating me so kindly. "Thanks," I croak. "I appreciate that."

He falls into another brooding silence that stretches into eternity.

"I love you," he rasps. "I never told you. I should have. I love you more than anything. I can't imagine my life without you, but I won't try to stop you from leaving. I just want you to be happy even if you can't do that with me."

Tears well up in my eyes. I can't see him, but I can't look at him anyway. "I love you, too!" I howl. "I don't want to leave.....I just don't know how to do any of this....."

He rushes over to my couch, sits next to me, and pulls me into his arms. "You don't have to do any of this. You don't have to do anything. You had a great life before. You'll get it again. All of this will be a distant memory. You don't have to worry about me or think about me or do anything for me. Just take care of yourself. Everything is going to work out. I promise."

He kisses me on the hair, but he makes sure never to kiss me anywhere near my face.

He finally pushes me upright so he can look at me. He rubs his hands up and down my arms and across my back, but he stays outside the bedspread. He never crosses that line.

"You don't have to sleep out here," he murmurs. "You take the bedroom."

"No," I choke. "I don't want to sleep in there. I'll stay here, at least for tonight."

He only nods. "Whatever you want. Whatever you need is fine with me." He kisses me on the forehead. "If I don't see you in the morning,

I'll see you when I get home from work and then I'll help you pack up your stuff to drive back. Okay?"

I nod. He stands up, walks away to the bedroom, and shuts the door with himself inside.

I collapse onto the couch and pull the bedspread over my head. This is the worst night of my life. I just need to shut my eyes and wake up tomorrow after all of this agony and heartache is behind me.

I wake up alone the next morning. I didn't hear Derek leave. He must have made quite an effort to slip out of the apartment without waking me up.

His consideration stabs me in the guts. He's doing everything possible to respect my decision. He doesn't try to talk me out of it.

I would like to believe he's doing that because he knows I'm right. That isn't the case, though. He still wants to work it out. He doesn't want me to leave at all.

He'll go through the whole procedure of moving me back to New Jersey. He'll do everything in his power to smooth the transition for me.

He'll do all of that even believing we still belong together. That on its own tells me what a good man he is. We just aren't right for each other.

I can't keep disintegrating here on the couch. I force myself to stand up, make the bed in the bedroom with the bedspread on it, take a shower, and put on real clothes.

I'm going to face the world with my head up. I'm going to bounce back from this no matter what. I won't let anyone stop me.

Maybe I'll get back into cooking once I move back to New Jersey. Maybe I'll cook for myself in ways I never have.

I could make all these gourmet dishes for myself just as easily as I made them for Derek. I could freeze the leftovers and take containers of leftovers to work for lunch. What's stopping me?

I go into the kitchen, but I just can't bring myself to take the containers Derek and I bought to use together. He might want to use them.

I can always get more from the container store. The whole world and the rest of my life lies before me full of potential and possibilities.

I go into the bedroom, tape up all the boxes I just dismantled from our move here, and start packing up my stuff.

I make up a bag to use over the next couple of days while I resettle into my apartment. I don't need anything else.

I work for two hours before I get a notification on my phone. It's an email from Alistair telling him that Derek contacted him.

Alistair insists I can get my old job back whenever I want it. I can even start on Monday if I want to.

He also tells me that Derek recommended me for David's old position. Alistair thinks it's a great idea, but he needs to run it by the executive board first.

He's certain they will agree based on my experience and my understanding of the company.

He says that, if I'm interested, I should start familiarizing myself with the computer system in the office and all the company procedures—which of course I already know.

I sit there staring at the phone. I'm not sure if I want to go that far, but I can't argue with the money.

I could do a lot with that salary. I could even afford to rent the apartment I used to share with Derek. I wouldn't have to live in my grungy old apartment.

I'll tell Derek to take me back to the newer, nicer apartment when he drives me. We have extra time on both places before our leases run out.

Chapter 28: Vivian

I tape up another box, carry it out to the living room, and start assembling another one when someone knocks on the apartment door.

I answer it and find three women standing there. "Um....can I help you?" I ask.

A tall, statuesque woman with long dark brown hair smiles at me. "I'm Samantha. We met last night at The Billionaires' Club gala. Remember?"

"Um....oh, yeah." I think I remember her, but I can't be certain. "Can I do anything for you?"

She waves at the two women standing next to her. One is an extremely petite, almost plain looking woman with straight mouse-brown, shoulder-length hair and the cheeriest smile I've ever seen.

The other is slightly taller and much curvier. They all wear casual clothes, but they all look unbelievably classy in a billionaire's-wife kind of way.

"This is Piper Lagrange and this is Melody Gottlieb," Samantha tells me. "They were both at the gala last night, too. Piper is Judah

Hayes's wife. Melody is married to Niko Holloway and I'm married to Lane Prince."

"Uh....yeah?" I ask. Why is she telling me this? Why are they even here?

"We saw you run out of the gala last night," Piper tells me. "We wanted to make sure you're okay."

"Derek told me about your decision to move back to New Jersey," Samantha adds. "Do you want any help packing?"

My shoulders slump. "No, I can get it. He didn't tell you to come here and talk me out of it, did he?"

"He didn't tell us anything," Melody replies. "We came because we wanted you to understand that you don't have to leave because you don't know anyone. We wanted to welcome you—and the gala obviously didn't work for you to do that."

"That's why we're here," Piper tells me. "We want to offer you our friendship and well wishes, even if it means just helping you pack up to leave." She peers behind me. "Are you sure you don't want any help? We're happy to chip in."

I heave a sigh and hold the door open. "I don't need any help, but you might as well come inside."

They come in and Samantha starts putting one of the flattened boxes back together. "You haven't started on the kitchen yet. Do you want me to do that?"

"Seriously," I tell her. "You guys don't need to do anything. I'll just keep working on the bedroom. Most of my stuff is in there."

They follow me into the bedroom and sit around while I put my shoes in another box.

"I don't blame you for running for the hills," Melody remarks from an armchair by the big bedroom windows. "I wanted to run for the hills when I first came around the club, too."

My head shoots up. "You did? But.....Derek said you were a member of the club. You're *in* the club."

She laughs and rolls her eyes. "I only joined a few months ago. I never had anything to do with business. I had to learn everything overnight when my father died." She blushes and wipes her hand across her brow. "I was a disaster. Believe me. I still am."

I can't stop staring at her. "You are?" She doesn't look like a disaster at all.

"She isn't the only one," Piper chimes in. "I never rubbed elbows with all those sharks before, either. I thought I was done for when I went to my first gala."

My eyes dart to her. "What happened? Why....but you.....you handled yourself so well last night.....you all did....."

"None of us was born to this," Samantha tells me. "Piper was just a middle-class layer before she got together with Judah."

"No way!" I exclaim.

"My first husband was a schoolteacher," Piper adds. "So that tells you right there what nobodies we were."

"I still make disastrous decisions every day," Melody goes on. "Samantha and some of the other women taught me a lot—and they still do. I'm just a newbie in this whole thing."

"I was in business, but I never went to any Billionaires' Club galas," Samantha chimes in. "I almost puked from nerves the first time I went with Lane."

I collapse on the bed and stare down at my hands. "I thought I was the only one."

Melody laughs. "You definitely aren't. I have to fight myself just to open my mouth around the other billionaires. I live in dread that I'm going to say the wrong thing and make a fool of myself."

"Every gala is a struggle," Piper tells me. "It's like the fashion designers of the world get together and try to come up with the dresses that will make the person wearing them as uncomfortable as possible."

The others burst out laughing. Their attitude switches something in my mind. "I....I thought I was the only one....."

Samantha's eyes twinkle at me. "You look tired. Why don't we go out for a drive? You said you're all right with packing everything on your own. Come on outside and get some fresh air. It will do you good and take your mind off all of this."

"Good idea," Melody adds. "Who could resist the chance to procrastinate?"

"I shouldn't," I hedge. "Derek is going to drive me back to New Jersey as soon as he finishes work. I want to be done and ready to go by the time he comes back—and I wouldn't want to just disappear and not be here when he comes back."

"We won't stay out too long," Samantha decides. "If he comes back early, we'll help you finish packing. We'll finish in no time and then you can go. Come on. You need to get out more. You've been stuck in this penthouse by yourself for way too long. No one can live like that."

The three women don't give me a chance to argue. They all stand up and head for the living room.

Don't ask me how they know I've been stuck in this penthouse by myself for way too long. Maybe it's written all over my face.

I follow them in a trance. Samantha is dead right. I can't even remember the last time I went out and just enjoyed myself with female friends. I hear about all these other women doing it, but that isn't a part of my life.

These women speak so easily about everything that bothered me last night. I can hardly bring myself to believe that those gorgeous, immaculately dressed women were as uncomfortable, nervous, and out of their depth as I was.

Piper holds the door open for me to walk out of the penthouse. This is the first time I've set foot outside it since Derek and I moved to New York. What in the world was I thinking?

The women all grin at me when we get into the elevator. "We're going out to play hooky," Melody snickers and the others giggle.

"We're kidnapping Vivian," Piper teases. "We're going to fly you away to our mothership."

I blush and wind up laughing. Their company heals something that was broken in my soul.

We ride down the elevator to the parking garage under the building. Samantha leads us to a classy BMW sedan parked across the garage from the elevator.

"This doesn't look like an alien mothership," I remark. "I feel cheated."

The others explode with laughter. "She's loosening up already," Piper remarks. "You sit in the back, Vivian. We can't trust you around the controls. You might blow up the planet."

We all pile into the car. Samantha gets behind the wheel, the engine roars to life, and she pulls out of the garage onto the street.

She starts driving through Manhattan and then gets onto the expressway. "Push the big red button!" she yells to Melody in the seat next to her.

"Not the big red button!" I scream.

They laugh. Melody leans forward and pushes a button on the dashboard. The button isn't red. The car roof unfolds and tucks in behind us. The car turns into a convertible.

The wind blows in all our faces. Melody raises her hands above her head and whoops. "Whoo!! Stand back, world!"

"Flag the mothership!" Piper yells from the back. "Tell the alien commanders we have our captive and she's ripe for experimentation!"

I can't help but laugh. "Now I'm getting worried."

"Where should we go?" Samantha calls over her shoulder.

"Don't go anywhere," Piper tells her. "Just drive around."

"Just don't go too far," Melody reminds them. "We have to take Vivian back at a reasonable hour."

"Forget it," I counter. "Who the hell cares, anyway?"

The others all hoot and laugh. "Listen to this!" Melody crows. "We're infecting her with our mind virus already!"

"What mind virus is that?" I ask.

"The mind virus that makes you forget your problems—at least until you go back home. It's the mind virus that lets you enjoy the moment and know that your problems will still be there waiting for you to solve them when you get back."

I look out at the city and let the wind blow through my hair. "Yeah. They will be."

"We're having fun here!" Melody yells. "We aren't here to talk or think about any problems." She points at Samantha. "Turn here. Let's see some scenery while we're out here."

Samantha turns off toward Long Island. We pass through the other boroughs and enter the suburbs. "I remember when I used to live somewhere like this," Piper remarks. "That was nice."

"I wish I could live somewhere like this," Melody adds. "Life would be a lot simpler."

"It is simpler," Piper tells her. "You and Niko could move out here. You could bake cookies and drive your kids to Little League."

Melody snorts. "When would I have time for that?"

"I like cooking." The words fall out of my mouth before I think to stop them.

Melody and Piper both spin around to stare at me. Samantha stares at me in the rearview mirror.

"You do?" Melody asks. "Are you any good?"

I nod. "I'm pretty good. It's always been a passion of mine."

"You have to give me some tips," she insists. "I'm hopeless."

Samantha snorts. "Don't listen to a word she says, Vivian. Melody is a really good cook. She learned from the cooks in her father's mansion when he wasn't watching."

"That doesn't mean I'm any good," Melody replies. "Besides, I don't have time to cook for Niko now. I'm too busy."

"What makes you think you would have time to learn from Vivian?" Samantha's hand shoots out. "Wow! Look at that!"

We all turn around to see what she's pointing at. I stare as the expressway leaves the suburbs and enters a much more rural part of Long Island.

Large estates and even a few farmhouses dot the surroundings.

I find myself staring at everything in wistful longing. This countryside brings back so many memories of my lost childhood.

"This is beautiful!" Piper breathes. "Imagine living somewhere like this."

"I grew up somewhere like this," I blurt out. "It was wonderful."

"You're so lucky!" Melody exclaims. "I'm so jealous."

"I always wanted to move somewhere like this so I could live the way I did when I was growing up. I just could never afford to buy a piece of land."

"Oooh! Look!" Samantha pulls over too fast. "This place is having an open home! Let's go take a look."

Chapter 29:
Vivian

S amantha pulls into a long driveway. It snakes up to a quaint farmhouse with flowerbeds, fences for animals, trees along the driveway, and even a small fruit orchard behind the house.

The realtor mills around inside with half a dozen other couples. The other three women and I pile out of the car and go inside to explore the place.

The house is old, but comfortable and well kept. All the garden space, orchard, and pastures look well taken care of, too.

I wander from the living room decorated with antique furniture to the bedrooms upstairs to the back kitchen door overlooking the orchard.

I stop there and gaze out over the surrounding countryside. I could have this. I could afford to buy a place like this on my salary if I took over as the head of Cast Iron Securities.

I make up my mind to do that. I won't move into Derek's old apartment. I'll stay where I am and start saving my money for the down payment on a piece of land.....a piece of land just like this one. This is perfect.

Samantha comes up behind me. "Imagine if you lived somewhere like this with Derek," she murmurs. "Would you want to stay in New York if you could live like this instead of in a high-rise penthouse?"

I spin around fast. "Are you serious?"

"Why not? You know he would buy this place for you in a flat second if you told him you wanted him to."

"But.....what about......?"

My head spins. All my plans.....I really don't want to go back to New Jersey. I don't want to leave Derek.

What if we could live somewhere like this? He wants that. He said so himself.

He could keep running his company from Midtown Manhattan. He could keep meeting with his friends from The Billionaires' Club.

I would be able to do so many things......

This is it. This is the place where it will happen. I can see myself cooking in that kitchen, growing my own food, and even starting a YouTube channel where I show everyone how I do things.

This place.....this house.....this land.....this is the key to it all. I can do all of that here. This place gives me the passion and motivation to do it all.

I want more than to do it. I can't wait to get started....but I have to wait. I have to make up with Derek first. I have to tell him about this place. That's going to be a completely different conversation.

The realtor comes over to us while we're standing there. He's a chunky guy of about thirty. "Can I answer any questions for you ladies?"

"How long has the house been on the market?" Samantha asks.

"About six months," he replies. "A lot of people come by and admire it, but not many have the time or energy a place like this really needs. I guess the right person hasn't come along who can give this place the love it deserves."

"Thank you," she tells him. "It's a beautiful property. I'm sure the right person will come along soon."

He smiles again and holds out his business card. "Call me any time if you need to know anything else or if you want to come back out and take a second look."

She thanks him, takes the card, and hands it to me. I can't even speak. I am not holding this card in my shaking hands.

I would never be able to afford a place like this—not in the middle of Long Island.

I would have to move out to the country somewhere in New Jersey or maybe even back to Pennsylvania before I found the right property.

I'll only be able to be the person who gives this property the love it deserves if I make up with Derek.

My soul thrills at the idea. I want that so bad, but maybe he won't want to. Maybe he won't want someone who keeps flip-flopping on him.

I'm not sure I can really go through with that. I'm too deep in thought to talk to the other women on our way back to Manhattan.

What will I tell Derek when he comes back? I really have no idea how I can face him—with any of this.

The women don't interrupt my thoughts. They chat amongst themselves, but they don't try to pull me back into their conversation. They already understand everything going on in my head.

How did this happen? How did I make three new friends without even trying?

I would spend a lot of time with them if I stayed here. I would see them at club galas, but I would see them other times, too.

We would raise our children together. We would share life's ups and downs.

I would finally have someone to talk to—someone other than Derek.

How did these women know I needed this so badly? I don't want to walk away from this any more than I want to walk away from him.

Will he be offended when I tell him that's another reason I want to stay—for the farmhouse and for these other people? What if he thinks I'm using him to get something when I don't really want him?

I do want him. That's the problem.

It isn't really a problem. I couldn't stay here when he was the only reason I stayed. That was the real problem. I had nothing else but him.

I would have so much more if I stayed. I would have the farm-house—and he said he wants that with me. Why not now? Why wait a dozen years?

Samantha parks in the garage. I come back to my senses when we climb out of the car and get into the elevator to ride upstairs.

"Are you going to be okay?" she asks on the way.

"We can stick around and hold Derek off with our pitchforks if you want us to," Melody offers and all four of us laugh.

"Something tells me that won't be necessary," I reply. "I really appreciate you guys stopping by. I really needed this."

Samantha beams at me. "You're welcome. Just call one of us if you need anything or if you just want to talk. You aren't alone. We all feel terrible that we let you think that."

"You definitely made up for it today." We stop outside the apartment and I hug each of them. "Thank you again."

They all smile at me, but right at that moment, my phone rings. I don't recognize the number.

I answer it and hold the phone to my ear. "Hello?"

"Is this Ms. Vivian Cooper?" a man's voice asks.

"Yes, I am Vivian Cooper."

"My name is Ashton Romaker. I'm the registrar at Mount Sinai Hospital in Manhattan. I'm sorry to tell you that your mother was just brought in by EMS half an hour ago. She suffered a massive stroke and she's in surgery right now. You're listed as her next of kin. It would be really helpful if you came down to the hospital as soon as humanly possible so you can consult with the doctors about her care."

"Uh....." I flounder for something to say. "Uh....okay.....I'm on my way right now."

I hang up and stare at the phone in stunned disbelief.

"What was that about?" Melody asks.

"Are you okay, Vivian?" Piper asks. "You look like it was something bad."

"My mother....." I stammer. "My mother.....she's in the hospital....she had a stroke...."

"Oh, my God!" Samantha gasps. "Come on! We have to go! I'll drive you! Get back in the elevator!"

We turn around. I can barely move. The women grab me to hustle me away, but right then, the elevator doors open and Derek comes out.

He slows when he sees all the women around me. "Um....what's going on?" he asks.

"Vivian's mother had a stroke," Samantha blurts out. "She's in the hospital. We were just about to drive her there."

Derek's features go hard and stony. "I'll drive her. Thank you all. I got this."

He takes hold of my elbow and pulls me into the elevator. I'm still standing there clutching my phone in brainless shock.

He keeps glancing at me. He doesn't ask if I'm okay or what I've been doing all day. He doesn't ask what I was doing with those women.

He finally asks, "Which hospital is she in?"

"Um....Mount Sinai....."

He only nods. The doors open in the parking garage and he puts me into the passenger seat of his Camry before he squeals out onto the street and takes off at high speed.

Chapter 30: Derek

I escort Vivian into the Mount Sinai Hospital lobby. We check in and find out that her mother is still in surgery upstairs.

We ride the elevator up to the stroke clinic where we have to wait in the waiting room for another three hours.

I don't mention taking her back to New Jersey. I leave a few different times to bring her coffee and snacks from the vending machines. We don't talk the whole time.

This isn't about me. I just need to be here for her in whatever way she needs me. I don't even care if we still break up after this.

She might need to stay in the penthouse for days or even longer until her mother gets healthy enough to leave the hospital. That's fine. I'll do whatever it takes so Vivian feels good about moving forward with her life.

I spend the time handling business on my phone. She stares into space in a blank stupor. I don't try to bring her back from that.

While I'm on the phone, I get an email from Alistair telling me the executive board has offered Vivian the head position at Cast Iron Securities to take my place. He's certain I'll understand considering everything that's been happening between us.

I tell him I'm happy for her and the company and that I'm sure she'll do an amazing job. I then tell him about her mother's illness and I don't know when Vivian will be ready to come back to town to start work. He offers his sympathies and tells me to tell her to take her time until she's ready.

I don't tell Vivian that. That can wait.

We're still sitting there when the doctors come out and ask if she's Vivian Cooper. She stands up to face the verdict.

"Your mother just came out of surgery," the doctor tells her.

"Is she going to be okay?" Vivian quavers.

"She made it through the surgery just fine, but after this, we're transferring her down to the poison control center. The stroke was caused by lead poisoning. Is it possible she became exposed somewhere? Her blood levels indicate a high concentration of lead in her bloodstream. We don't usually see cases like this unless the person has been exposed over a long period of time."

"I...I don't know how she could have gotten exposed to it," Vivian stammers. "She never goes anywhere—except when I take her to the park a couple of times a week. She stays in her apartment the rest of the time."

"How modern is her apartment?" the doctor asks.

She cringes. "You know....it isn't modern. It's all I can afford while paying all of her expenses and mine. It isn't much, but it works."

The doctor only nods. "Then it's likely the apartment has lead paint and she got exposed that way. If the paint is old and flaking, the dust can get into the air and settle in people's lungs and in their food so they ingest it. You'll need to strip the paint from the walls, and for that, you need to go through all the health and safety protocols for your area. You should contact your city council and poison control center to get all the information."

"But.....the apartment is a rental," she points out. "Shouldn't the landlord pay for that?"

"Yes, of course. In that case, you should contact the landlord about it. In the meantime, your mother will undergo special treatment to detoxify her blood and chelate the lead out of her system. She'll probably stay in the hospital for three or four days before she's healthy enough to be released."

He leaves. Vivian turns around slowly, but she doesn't see anything, not even me. She barely notices when I put my arm around her.

"We'll find her another place to live," I murmur in her ear. "I'll help you. Don't worry. She doesn't have to go back to that apartment."

"You don't understand...." she blurts out, but right then, a different hospital person comes up to us.

This one is a middle-aged lady carrying a tablet in one hand. "Ms. Cooper? I just need to get your insurance information to cover your mother's care."

"Um....." Vivian looks around in another panicked trance.

"Doesn't your insurance from Cast Iron Securities cover it?" I ask.

She wrings her hands and her features spasm. "I'm not an employee of Cast Iron Securities anymore! I quit and I haven't restarted! The insurance won't cover an ailment that occurred outside the coverage window."

I lay my hand on her arm to calm her down and answer the woman over my shoulder. "I'll pay for it. You can send the bills to me." I give her my email address and all my other contact information.

She leaves. Now I have to deal with Vivian.

She stands there shifting her weight from one foot to the other and looking everywhere but at me. Her eyes swim with terror and confusion.

"Take it easy now," I murmur. "Everything is going to be okay. I'll take care of it. You don't have to worry about anything. I got this."

"You don't understand, Derek!" she practically shrieks.

"Explain it to me." I try to keep my voice from shaking. I've never seen her like this. This is terrible. "Just tell me what you need. You know I'll do anything you need me to do."

"Derek.....I need you to.....I need to......"

I wait, but she can't get the words out.

I pull her down into the waiting room chairs. I can't stop myself from putting my arm around her. "Just take a minute to calm down," I murmur in her ear. "You're upset over this, but it will pass. You'll deal with this and you'll go on taking care of your mother. Alistair just contacted me. The executive board is offering you the head position at Cast Iron Securities. You're going to make enough money to take care of your mother. You don't have to worry about anything."

"Derek.....I need to tell you something....."

"Anything, sweetheart." I can hardly make myself heard. "You know I would do anything for you."

"I need you.....to......" She gulps. "I need you to......drive me.....to Long Island.....I need.....to show you.....something there.....something important......I can't tell you now.....I have to show you."

I stiffen in my chair. What could she possibly want to show me on Long Island?

I shrug that off. "Okay, sweetie. Whatever you need. Let's go."

I lead her back down to the parking garage, put her in my car, and start driving. I have no idea where we're going or what will happen when we get there. I hope it isn't anything worse than what we're already going through.

I don't hold out any hope that this will change anything. Maybe she just needs to get out of Manhattan and drive around to clear her head.

I make the same decision for the thousandth time today to accept whatever outcome she thinks is best. I resign myself to the inevitable that she'll leave me and go back to her own life.

I can't argue with it if she really thinks that's what's best for her. I can't force her to stay with me if she sets her mind to leave.

I get lost in my own thoughts when she points to one side. "Over there," she tells me. "Pull into the driveway."

I turn into a random driveway. That's when I realize where we are.

The driveway ends at an old character farmhouse surrounded by fields, trees, orchards, and garden beds.

A single car sits in the driveway in front of the house. I pull in next to it and switch off the engine.

Vivian sits next to me in silence. She doesn't say a word. She doesn't have to.

I stare at the house as the truth sinks in. This is it. This is the house. I understand without her explaining anything to me.

This is why she couldn't stay with me—not at the penthouse. That place had a repulsive effect on her. It threw her out. She never could live there. It's a miracle she lasted as long as she did.

This is it. This is the answer to it all. This is what she's been trying to tell me since the beginning.

She would never be happy living anywhere else. She never had a problem with me. She couldn't stay with me because she didn't have this—the one thing she most needs.

I see it all when I look at the house and the land. It's close enough to Manhattan that I can keep running my business from there. I don't have to change anything.

I'll have to drive to work every morning, but who cares about that?

My life looks a whole lot different here. This house is a home in ways no apartment ever could be.

I've lived in some of the most luxurious penthouses in the world. None of them was a home—not like this.

This is what she needs. She needs a home. This is why she's been so exhausted and stressed all these years. She needs to go home. Now it's up to me to take her there.

A man comes out of the house and looks at us through the windshield. He carries a business folio in one hand and a stack of papers in the other. He looks like a real estate agent.

I leave Vivian where she is and get out of the car to go talk to him. I hold out my hand to shake his. "Hi," I tell him. "I'm seriously interested in buying this place."

His eyebrows shoot up. "Don't you want to take a look around first?"

"Yes, I do, but I'm seriously interested. I want any information you can give me about the property."

"Um...okay....." He scrambles to unzip his folio and hands me a sheaf of papers stapled together. "It's all in there. I was just about to leave, but I can wait while you take a look around." He glances toward the car. "Is that your wife? She and her friends stopped by earlier today."

I decide to skip the explanation. "Yeah, she is. She loves this place and really wants it, so we're going to go for it. I'll just take a few minutes and come right back out."

He nods and goes to put his stuff in his car. I enter the house. It's as charming and comfortable on the inside as it looks on the outside. It creaks in all the right places like a person talking to me.

I take a brief tour through the house and flip through the papers he gave me. I take one look at the sale price and make up my mind.

I go back outside and meet up with him. He's leaning against his fender. "We'll take it," I tell him. "I want to make an offer for the asking price."

His eyes fly open again. "Great! That's wonderful."

I give him my email address. "Send me through the purchase agreement and we'll set the whole thing up." I jerk my thumb over my shoulder. "Do you mind if we spend some time here? We might be a while. I don't know if you want to leave or what."

"Take all the time you need. Enjoy yourselves."

"Thanks." I go over to the car, open the passenger door, and offer Vivian my hand.

She takes it, but she won't look at me when I lift her to her feet.

I lead her into the house. We migrate from the living room to the kitchen to the pantry and finally upstairs to the bedrooms.

I stop in the middle of the master bedroom. The windows look out over the surrounding pasture.

The room doesn't have an in-floor jacuzzi. It has one queen-sized four-poster bed and some nice antique furnishings. That's all.

This house isn't luxurious at all. It has a hard-working, almost dirty air to it that feels so, so comfortable and inviting.

No one has to work hard to make this house a home. Heaven only knows how many generations of families have grown up here.

I turn to Vivian. Her eyes overflow with questioning and emotion when she looks up at me with all her heart pouring out to me.

God, I love her! She's my future. She's my heart and soul. We're going to build a beautiful life here—but it will be so different from the life we would have had in Manhattan.

I'm sure I'll be the first and last member of the Billionaires' Club who lives like this—and I love that. I can't wait to roll up my sleeves and learn how to do all of this.

No one is better able to teach me all of that than Vivian. I can't wait to become her first and most attentive student.

I stick my hand in my pants pocket and touch the box I've been carrying around for days.

I planned to propose to her after the gala before everything blew up in my face. I've been carrying the ring around in my pocket ever since.

I didn't want to ask because I didn't want to pressure her into changing her mind about us.

Now I know it's right. This is the moment—the perfect time. The house makes it all work out for the best.

I sink onto one knee, pull out the box, and open it in front of her. "Marry me," I whisper. "Marry me and live here with me forever. Don't ever leave. I can't live without you. We'll bring your mother to live here with us for as long as she has left. Let me give you the life of your dreams. Let me take all your cares off your shoulders. I never want you to worry about anything ever again. Just stay and marry me."

Tears overflow her eyes and she holds out her hand to me. "Yes!" she chokes. "Yes, I'll marry you!"

I can't stop my heart from pounding when I slip the ring onto her finger. It's happening. It's all coming true.

She bursts out in excited laughter when I kiss her knuckles, stand up, and fold my arms around her. This woman is mine. All my dreams are going to come true in her and through her.

I lean back and kiss her, but her presence makes me too emotional. I can't even begin to touch her. She's too precious even for that.

I take her hand, sit down on the bed, and pull her down next to me.

I burst out in excited laughter, too, when I look at her and see her beaming up at me. "Welcome home, sweetheart," I tell her.

She laughs again. "Did you buy it?"

"I just talked to the realtor. He's going to send me the paperwork?"

She bounces on the mattress and giggles. "Yay! I can't wait!"

"So you came out with Samantha and the others," I remark. "Did they plan this?"

"No, they stopped by to offer me their friendship and to help me pack. Then they said we should go for a drive just to take my mind off everything. Samantha spotted this place and we pulled in just to take a look." She looks away. "It all sort of went downhill from there."

I laugh again. Nervous excitement keeps me glued to the edge of my seat.

I keep squeezing her hand and feeling the ring there. "You're going to have to teach me how to do all of this," I tell her. "I don't know anything."

She beams at me and then kisses me. "Don't worry. You can learn by watching my YouTube channel."

I laugh again. "That's perfect."

Epilogue: Vivian

I sit in the front row of the audience hall and applaud with the rest of the guests. Kevin Drake stands on the stage at the front of the room.

He gives a speech into the microphone about how Derek worked his way up to building one of the wealthiest financial asset companies in New York, lost it all, and then did the same thing a second time.

Kevin calls Derek up to the stage, shakes his hand, hands him a decorative shield commemorating this moment, and announces to the audience that Derek is now a member of The Billionaires' Club.

This is a small gathering closed to the public. No one is here except the other billionaires and their spouses.

That's enough. The rest of the world doesn't need to know about this.

The press has already been making a big deal about Whirling Investment Assets' meteoric rise to the top. The other billionaires in the club have had plenty to do with that, but none of them can stop talking about Derek.

He beams and waves from the stage taking in all the praise and admiration of his peers. He's one of them now. He's back on their level where he belongs.

I couldn't be happier for him, now that I see him getting everything he ever wanted. He's happier and more content than I've ever seen him.

I'm happier and more content than I've ever been before, too. I'm getting everything I ever wanted, thanks to him.

The life of my dreams waits for me outside this hall. Oh, what am I saying? This is the life of my dreams. This is part of it—seeing him achieve his dreams, too.

He leaves the stage and the gathering breaks up into another loose collection of conversations. Servers and caterers pass through the crowd handing out champagne and food to everyone.

I wind up talking to a bunch of different people, including the women and also plenty of the men.

I know almost everyone in here now and they know me. They credit me with Derek making it back, but I understand what they aren't saying.

They know I'm the reason he's happy. He wouldn't be happy if he got his wealth back without all the rest of our life outside his business.

He's happy at the farmhouse. He's much happier there than he was at the penthouse or even at our apartment in New Jersey.

He works hard and learns even harder. He does everything with massive energy. He gets more done in the time he takes off from his business than most people get done in a month.

He shoulders his way out of the crowd to join up with me, puts his arm around me, and kisses me in front of everyone. They all know we're engaged.

We stand together while we finish talking to our friends. Then it's time to go home.

He brings the car around and opens my door to let me get inside. He drives a new black Bentley—but only when he comes to Manhattan for business or some event like this.

The rest of the time, he drives his new black silver pickup truck. He uses that to bring in supplies for the farmhouse.

I slip my hand into his lap while he drives. "I'm so proud of you," I tell him. "You're a man any woman would be proud of."

He shoots me a grin on the side. "I saw you out there holding court with everyone. You really owned the room. I'm proud of you, too. You stepped up and slew that dragon like nobody's business."

I laugh. "I can't believe I put all those people so high on a pedestal. They're all so....so normal."

He joins in the joke. "So are we. You're going to marry a billionaire and we're normal people."

I squeeze his hand. "I'm glad. I wouldn't want us to be anything else."

He pulls into the farmhouse driveway. The headlights swivel across the house and then switch off when he shuts the car down.

He takes my hand on the way into the dark house. He switches on the lights.

We're in the process of cleaning out and renovating the space under the stairs to make more storage room.

The previous owners left that space packed with junk. We have to go through it all, decide what is worth saving and what isn't, and then build some shelves in there.

I go upstairs, take off my ball gown, and change into my around-the-house jeans and a T-shirt knotted at the waist.

I come downstairs to see Derek putting his shield on the mantel shelf in the living room. He stands there with his back to the room while he stares at the shield and adjusts its position again and again.

I don't make a sound. I don't want to disturb him.

This moment means a lot to him. He doesn't have to explain it to me. He said he would walk away from Whirlwind Investment Assets if I wanted him to.

I don't believe he could have done that even if he tried. He couldn't give up such an important part of his life.

He turns around suddenly and blushes when he sees me. "Sorry," he mumbles.

"Don't apologize. You have every right to be proud of yourself." I kiss him and go kneel in front of a box by the stairs. "You know what this means, don't you?"

"What does it mean?" he asks.

"It means now you have to start working toward two billion."

He laughs and heads for the other end of the stairs. "I think it means I need to change my clothes and get back to work."

He heads upstairs. I stay where I am and go through another box of random, dusty knickknacks.

I wait until I hear his footsteps coming back. They pace across the upstairs landing, down the stairs, and he stops in front of me.

He holds up the home pregnancy test I left on his side of the bed. It's positive.

"What the hell is this?!" he husks.

"You can see what it is, darling," I tell him. "I'm pregnant."

He gapes at me blinking extra slowly. His lips move, but no sound comes out.

He stares at me in shocked horror when I stand up and walk toward him. This is the ultimate ending to our story—the story of how we got together.

Now another story is starting—a story as old as time and just as sweet.

I stop in front of him to wait for him to wrap his mind around what is happening to us.

He reacts too fast, grabs me, and pulls me in. He laughs, gasps, and sobs in my ear all at the same time. He crushes me in an iron hold that will never break.

We're embarking on the next adventure. It will probably be as rocky and nerve-racking as the last one, but we're as ready as we're ever going to be.

We'll build a home and make it a good one. Nothing could be better than that.

End of Book 4.

Keep Reading

The Billionaires' Club Series: Book 5: Forever Young

Dante Helme might be one of the oldest billionaires in The Billionaires' Club, but he's also one of the strongest, sharpest, and most dangerous. Everyone respects him for his knowledge and experience, but also for his tireless energy, youthful enthusiasm, and dedication to helping his friends and family succeed.

Dante's world gets turned upside down when he falls for a woman a third his age and he winds up in a competitive love triangle with his own son. Something has to give and it won't be pretty when it does.

When worlds collide and the heart takes over, someone will ride off into the sunset with everything they ever wanted. Someone else will be left in pieces with nothing.

You can find it at your favorite book retailer.

Get All of AE Moran's Free Books

S ign Up Once—Get all A.E. Moran's free books including brand new releases

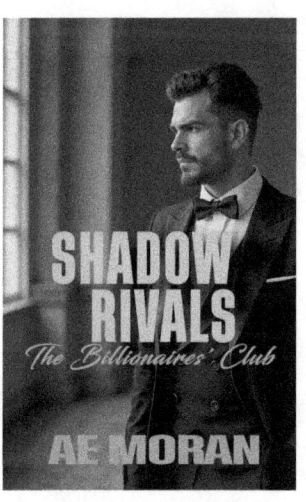

Holden Seager is hot, magnetic, and filthy, stinking, obscenely rich. He commands a room the minute he walks in the door. So what happens when meets another shark as powerful, as charismatic, and as successful as he is—not to mention ten years younger? When these two meet across the negotiating table, one of them will walk away the undisputed winner. The other will walk away with nothing.

Or so it seems.

Unless they're best friends.

When the business deal of a lifetime falls flat on its face and neither of these titans knows how to bring it back to life, this might be the opportunity Dayna Turner has been waiting for.

There's just one problem. She works as an assistant to one of these powerful men....and she's in love with the other. It's a recipe for disaster and heartbreak—unless Dayna can pull off an even bigger coup that will leave them all richer, happier, and more closely connected than ever. The alternative is the destruction of everything all three of them have worked so hard to build.

Sign up at www.authoraemoran.com to read it for free.

About AE Moran

A .E Moran is the contemporary romance pen name for Theo Mann.

I write 70 books per year—and yes, before you ask, all these books are my original creative work. Nothing written under my name is AI-generated or ghostwritten because I write better than AI and any ghostwriter out there.

People don't read fiction for entertainment or to escape from reality. People read fiction to see their humanity reflected in another person's character and story.

This is my promise to you. When you read my books, you'll see your own humanity reflected in the characters and stories. I take this commitment to my readers very seriously. My books are an intimate form of communication between us. I would never disrespect my readers by turning that over to a machine or another writer. This is my bond between me and you as my reader.

I write 20,000 words per day as my daily work output. If anyone with a public platform would like to challenge me to prove this in a controlled environment, feel free to contact me on this website's contact page.

I worked as a professional ghostwriter for fifteen years. Now I'm going for the Guinness World Record by writing 700 books over the next ten years and 1400 books over the next twenty years, all originally written by me. See my website for the full book list.

I'm also the author of *Proof for the Existence of God* and the *Crimes Against Fiction* blog. You can find all my nonfiction work at www.crimes-against-fiction.com.

If you have a story idea, or if you would like me to explore a series in more depth, or if you'd like me to explore a character by writing a spinoff series about that character or world, leave me a message on my website's contact page. I answer all reader emails, so ask me anything, tell me what you liked and didn't like, and let me know where you'd like your favorite series to go. I would love to hear your ideas and find out what you'd like to read next.

You can find out more at www.theomann.com or at www.authoraemoran.com.

Also by AE Moran (so far)